W9-AVD-736

Endless River

Other Five Star Titles
by Elizabeth Fackler:

Patricide
When Kindness Fails

Endless River

Elizabeth Fackler

Five Star • Waterville, Maine

FIC
Fac

Copyright © 2005 by Elizabeth Fackler

All rights reserved.

This novel is a work of fiction. Names, characters, places and incidents are either the product of the author's imagination, or, if real, used fictitiously.

No part of this book may be reproduced or transmitted in any form or by any electronic or mechanical means, including photocopying, recording or by any information storage or retrieval system, without the express written permission of the publisher, except where permitted by law.

First Edition, Second Printing

Published in 2005 in conjunction with Tekno Books and Ed Gorman.

Set in 11 pt. Plantin by Christina S. Huff.

Printed in the United States on permanent paper.

Library of Congress Cataloging-in-Publication Data

Fackler, Elizabeth.
    Endless river / by Elizabeth Fackler.—1st ed.
        p.   cm.
        ISBN 1-59414-270-X (hc : alk. paper)
        1. Teenage boys—Crimes against—Fiction.   2. Mothers and daughters—Fiction.   3. Ex-police officers—Fiction.
    4. Teenage girls—Fiction.   5. Kidnapping—Fiction.   I. Title.
    PS3556.A28E53 2005
        813′.54—dc22
                                                    2004062489

Endless River

This story is based on a true crime.

Author's Note

I would like to thank the staff of the Roswell Public Library for their help in researching the original kidnapping, and the many friends and contemporaries who shared their memories of the event. Also Detective S. of the Roswell Police Department, who asked to remain anonymous.

Chapter One

Idly watching yellow leaves fall from the spreading mulberry between her and the adobe wall on the alley, seventeen-year-old Amy Sterling was standing in front of her kitchen sink eating cereal when she saw her mother's tenant come through the back gate after his morning run. His tanned chest glittered with sweat as he peeled off his soaked T-shirt and stood appraising the height of the grass. It was due to be mowed, a chore he performed as part of his rent, and she almost wished she could stay and watch. Since learning he and her mother were lovers, she had been fascinated by nearly every move he made.

It had been exactly a week ago that she discovered their affair. Coming home early because of a bomb threat at school, she had been eager to finish the blouse she was making as a challenge to the school's newly imposed dress code. Red or black shirts and black or khaki slacks, tailored in totally unprovocative styles, were the rule, but she meant to push the administration's tolerance of flamboyance with her intimately contoured red silk blouse.

Certain Mr. Shane would single her out for admonishment, she blushed to admit she was called voluptuous, which by current standards meant plump. At five-five, she weighed a hundred and thirty pounds, a full ten of which she would swear were her breasts. Her mother had gone so far as to buy her a fifty-dollar minimizer bra. It flattened and held her firm, but what it didn't do for her projection it did for her cleavage. Low cut blouses definitely caught the eye of any straight boy in range, and an adult like Mr. Shane was even more fun because his job required he see her as a child.

By her reckoning, he was probably about the same age as her mother's tenant, anything over thirty being equal until a person hit dotage, which these days seemed to fall at whim. The principal and the tenant were close to the same height, too—just under six feet—but while Mr. Shane was willowy, Devon Gray was a taut bundle of muscles he maintained with discipline. She had seen him doing curls with weights, his biceps slithering beneath skin the color of saddle-soaped leather. She had also seen the weight bench in his room, though she hadn't been inside.

Painted yellow with a red tile roof like the house she lived in with her mother, the converted stucco garage sat at the end of the concrete driveway along the edge of their back yard. From the street, Devon had to open a gate in the white picket fence, then walk along a corrugated brick path to his front door, which had been inserted between two windows in the long side of the former garage. The windows were covered with wooden shutters on the inside, but he had left them open that day when he went downtown, and she peeked in.

Other than the weight bench, a radio, and a couple of books whose titles she couldn't read from so far away, the room hadn't changed. The same autumn landscape of the Hondo Valley was on the wall, the same oval rag rug in front of the sofa that folded out to make a bed. It was on that bed where she later saw Devon and her mother making love. Lucinda had been on top, her slender body elfin-looking astride the man, the short cut of her auburn hair doing nothing to hide her earnest expression.

Amy couldn't remember ever having seen her mother naked. To see her mother's breasts for the first time as they were being fondled by a man caused her world view to tumble into a new configuration. Not only was the joining of their groins a darkly shadowed juncture Amy could almost smell, her mother's head was thrown back and her face rigid with concentration, while the man was playfully smiling as if he were pleased. Amy had never considered that a man would smile like that during sex. No one did in the movies. There a man's mouth was either as contorted as if he were enduring a difficult bowel movement, or his lips were slathered on the woman's so no expression could be discerned. Devon Gray seemed to be admiring something he didn't quite consider his doing, and the humility of his participation made Amy curious about how Nathan would smile beneath her in bed.

Only yesterday, when Nathan hugged her at school, she had felt his erection and been so embarrassed she pushed him away. Now she found the prospect more interesting, as if seeing her mother and Devon gave her permission to investigate such tantalizingly bizarre behavior for herself. Witnessing what she had also made her look at Devon differently. The other night when she watched him check the oil in his old brown pickup, she observed his hands slide the dipstick in, pull it out and wipe it clean, then slide it in again, and she couldn't help thinking of those same hands on her mother's breasts. Feeling uneasy around him wasn't new, and becoming aware of his sexuality didn't alleviate that, but being privy to his affair with her mother helped Amy accept him as an ally. As if any harm he could inflict, and she suspected it might be significant, would now be marshaled in their defense.

Both she and Lucinda had known from the day he inquired about renting the apartment that he had been a cop in El Paso. The way he told it, he simply got burned out after ten years on what anyone would call an onerous job. Probably because she also had experience with burnout, Lucinda had accepted his explanation without inquiring further. Amy, however, suspected he had been in trouble in Texas. The state line was only a hundred miles south, El Paso itself barely a four-hour drive, which put him far enough away to change jurisdictions yet close enough to buy the *El Paso Times* the same day it was published, something she noticed he usually did.

When she discussed her theory with her mother, Lucinda admitted Berrendo was a town where people could easily disappear. As long as they were law-abiding and generally quiet, they blended in with hardly a ripple. But she scoffed at Amy's notion that Devon was hiding out.

Amy watched him go inside his garage apartment. After putting her bowl and spoon in the dishwasher, she picked up her books on her way out the back door, and left for school.

Devon watched his landlady's daughter walk down the driveway on her platform sneakers, the mass of her long dark hair swaying with her gait. Although her color scheme complied with the school's dress code, her red silk blouse clinging to the generous curves of her breasts above a pair of tight black jeans radiated the eager sexuality of an unseasoned hooker. He wondered why young women aligned sexual freedom with presenting themselves as whores, often dead ones at that, with their eggplant lipstick beneath faux-bruised eyes. But most of all, Amy's sexual ripeness made him suspect he might come to regret sleeping with her mother.

Lucinda insisted her daughter wasn't aware of the shift in their relationship, but Devon had seen a difference in Amy as soon as the change occurred. She watched him more intently, a puzzle behind her eyes. When he mentioned it to Lucinda, she credited it to Amy's curiosity about his past, making him quickly change the conversation's direction. Aware of Amy's curiosity from the beginning, he was surprised Lucinda wasn't more inquisitive about why a former homicide detective had taken up residence in her garage apartment. Retirement was a bit suspicious for a man who hadn't yet seen forty and had no financial assets other than a house in El Paso and a brown Dodge pickup ten years past its prime.

It was loneliness that had driven him to allow Lucinda into his bed. He hoped she understood that and wasn't counting on something beyond his ability to give. Knowing most single women craved marriage, he also knew any commitment would be hollow coming from a man on the run. He liked her, though; liked her daughter and their yellow stucco house with its snug back yard under the shade of a giant mulberry tree. Liked the gentle climate of the Pecos Valley and living in a town small enough that its lights didn't block out the stars at night. Liked the quiet rhythm of his days, working out with weights, tending the lawn, walking downtown for a newspaper and breakfast in Denny's on 2nd and Main, where the waitresses flirted with him while the other loners at the counter mumbled into their empty cups. He also liked prowling the valley at night, driving past dark pecan orchards sheltering pronghorn antelope, dairies fragrant with fresh manure, and fields fecund with impending harvest. Liked Lucinda enticing him into bed on her afternoons off, and Amy chatting while he tinkered under the hood of his truck. But the girl crackling with unfulfilled sex and the woman lolling in the laziness after orgasm were two pillars holding a tightrope he hadn't intended to walk.

After mowing the lawn and taking a shower, Devon sat at Denny's counter with the local paper while waiting for his eggs-over-easy to come out of the kitchen. When he turned to the obituary page and saw that the ex-sheriff of a nearby county had died, Devon couldn't resist a smile, though it wasn't the death that tickled him. It was the fact that Roy Rinkle had been known as the singing sheriff because he favored his inmates with songs from Broadway shows, songs he himself sang. The one and only time Devon had any dealings with Rinkle—picking up a thief to transport back to El Paso—the sheriff had graced the transfer of custody with "Some Enchanted Evening," a sentiment the prisoner hadn't appreciated though Devon had been amused.

Meeting the eyes of the man on the next stool killed Devon's urge to share the joke. He hadn't seen the man before, though that wasn't unusual, as the restaurant was known to attract drifters. This one gave off the acrid odor of fear-induced sweat that made Devon's instincts scream an alert he was powerless to act on. He took his newspaper and coffee to the nearest empty booth.

With a sneer that camouflaged how scared he felt, Buck Powell watched the man move to a booth. Though the man had been smiling when he looked over, something he saw had changed his expression to a wary readiness that made Buck decide to steer clear of him. Which wouldn't be hard since it was time Buck made his play, past time in fact, and here he sat staring at coffee he didn't want because he already felt too hot. He wished he had gone into a bar or bought a bottle somewhere, but he didn't trust himself to take only the one shot he needed. Any more would impair his performance, and then there was the fact that he couldn't hope to impersonate a cop if he walked into the situation drunk.

By the time he left Denny's it was ten-thirty, which meant school had been in session two and a half hours. He had been trying to outwait the guy in the booth, not wanting to attract attention because he felt certain the guy was

14

among the brotherhood of cops. They had a way of watching the world matched only by criminals. Buck knew the look well: the penetrating focus of a predator. But the cop wouldn't leave. After dawdling with his breakfast, then flirting with the waitress when she took his empty plate, he laid the local paper aside and opened the *El Paso Times*, apparently intending to read every page over what must have been his fifth cup of coffee.

Buck's second cup was still full. The waitress had long ago quit offering more, having caught on that he was waiting. The counter at Denny's was famous for being occupied by bums with nowhere to go. Despite his physical proximity at the moment, Buck rarely put himself in their company. Today he was dressed up, wearing a navy blue sports coat and sky blue tie, his yellow cotton shirt and khaki pants having been pressed at the cleaners. He had even shined his shoes and gotten himself a hair cut. But compared to the cop in the booth—a man wearing a white T-shirt under a brown corduroy jacket and a pair of faded Levi's—Buck knew he wouldn't pass for a peace officer in the eyes of anyone whose life depended on being able to spot one.

When he finally got up to pay for his coffee and leave, he felt the cop's eyes follow him all the way out the door and along the sidewalk to the parking lot. Even then he could feel himself being watched as he unlocked the door of the green Pontiac that Zeb bought for this job. A '91 station wagon with parking decals from some college in Colorado cluttering its back window, in Buck's opinion the Pontiac was a flag announcing the location of the culprit. At least it would be when the caper was history. Right now was still set-up, which made the car obscure for the moment. But it wasn't a vehicle Buck could keep as payment for helping Zeb pull this off. Having hoped for something he could feel proud to own, Buck figured the Pontiac's future lay in one of those junkyards littering the desert east of El Paso.

Sitting on 2nd at the red light on Main, he glanced into Denny's and saw the cop still watching him. Their gazes meshed for an instant, then the cop looked back at his paper as if he were reading. Buck cursed himself for not having turned west when he left the lot and avoiding this intersection. It wouldn't have been more than a block or two out of his way. Instead here he squirmed like a virgin on her honeymoon, pinned under the cop's nose. Buck hoped the cop was retired or on vacation or something and just passing through. In any case not an active member of the local department, whose every officer would be looking for this Pontiac in another few hours.

Finally the light changed and Buck escaped the intersection. A block farther east, he turned right on Pecos Avenue, traveled south all the way to Hobbs, then turned west toward the high school. Sweating again, he turned on the radio and twisted the dial until he heard Springsteen's "Born in the U.S.A." He cranked the volume and sang along. When he saw the school ahead on his left, he smiled at himself in the rearview mirror. "Cool, calm, and meaner'n shit," he muttered, slashing his palm down on the stick of the turn signal. The little green arrow started clicking off the pain-free seconds left to the arrogant s.o.b. who'd had the nerve to cross Cousin Zeb.

Lucinda was the librarian-in-charge, so the problem was hers. Mrs. Peckham had come to the reference desk with a decidedly unpleasant expression on her squashed little face. Nodding her head toward the magazine area, she pursed her lips, widened her eyes, and managed to appear simultaneously alarmed and disapproving. Lucinda didn't need to look at the young man in the reading area to know his offense. She smiled at Mrs. Peckham, whose upturned nose looked like a collapsed button in the middle of her face, her tiny eyes like specks of blue glass nestled in a pink powdered pillow, her red mouth glistening with gloss.

"I'm sorry, Mrs. Peckham," Lucinda said softly, "but this is a public building and he has a legal right to be here."

"Dead cats smell better than he does," the old woman whispered.

Lucinda glanced his direction, chagrined to see him trying not to listen. "I wish I could say he'll be gone soon, but he usually spends all day when he comes."

"Then I'll be gone," Mrs. Peckham answered. "It's a shame tax-paying citizens are driven from the library we generously support by some ne'er-do-well who hasn't the decency to take a bath!"

Lucinda watched the wide-beamed woman waddle to the circulation desk where Yolanda greeted her with a less than enthusiastic smile. The clerk looked over Mrs. Peckham's head to give Lucinda a conspiratorial grin, which told her that despite her efforts to be quiet the conversation had been heard. She again glanced at the young offender, but he appeared to be engrossed in the magazine he held.

He wasn't unattractive, and he seemed intelligent and had been articulate whenever he approached the reference desk to ask for help, which made her wonder how his circumstances had been so diminished as to necessitate him spending his nights outside and begging whatever meals he managed to get. She knew he did those things because he carried a sleeping bag tied to the bottom of his knapsack and because she had seen him coming out of the Salvation Army's soup kitchen more than once. Since it was on her route home, she passed it often enough that even the transients who didn't patronize the library looked familiar. The soup kitchen also offered beds and baths, but apparently this young man wasn't interested in availing himself of more than their food.

Although she had never asked his name, she frequently found herself defending his right to use the library. In a case famous within the profession, a Rastafarian who sued a public library in New Jersey for kicking him out because of his body odor had won enough money that he was no longer a transient. Berrendo was a small town and couldn't afford such a lawsuit. But beyond that, Lucinda felt sorry for the young man and thought if more people treated him kindly he might be inclined to return the favor by occasionally taking a bath. Once a week would make his scent as palatable as many of the society matrons who swamped themselves with perfume.

Eleven o'clock. She could go home in an hour if her relief showed up on time. Having previously disliked this split weekend of half-days on Fridays and Mondays, she smiled, thinking working Saturdays was much more appealing now that she spent her free weekday afternoons with Devon.

Yolanda wheeled a cart of books to be shelved past the reference desk, turning up her nose in sympathy with Mrs. Peckham. Lucinda laughed silently at the modest joke, then looked at the offender again, wondering where his parents were and how they could have let him come to such a state.

His name was Peter Rechauser, he was twenty-two years old, and his parents in Detroit were gnawed by worry over where he was and what he was doing. Since trading home for the road, he called himself simply Pete Reck. The various soup kitchens he availed himself of often asked, occasionally another transient would feel friendly enough to need a handle to call him by, and the ubiquitous police always wanted a name, home address, and place of employment. Pete's stock answer was that he slept in the open while looking for an opportunity. Neither of those was a lie, but the opportunity he watched for was a chance to divert some piece of worldly goods to his personal use.

He didn't consider himself a thief since he didn't steal for profit but survival. A pilfered loaf of bread, package of bologna, and quart of milk was a feast. To get his greens, he grazed in the produce sections of grocery stores. Dumpster diving provided his main sustenance, though sometimes he got away with wandering through a restaurant and picking leftovers off plates on tables not yet bussed. Most of his food procuring methods resulted in his being thrown out, usually with loud threats and curses, sometimes physical violence. The accumulated effect served to make him slink even when he wasn't breaking a law, so he lived like a criminal though, in his opinion, his only offense was poverty.

Keeping clean was a constant challenge. In the summer he could usually find a creek or river to wash in, but now that the year was turning toward winter, they were cold enough to give a man pneumonia when the sun was down. When it was up, he risked arrest for indecent exposure. Public restrooms carried the same liability, especially those in libraries because a child could enter unexpectedly. Any sexual affront to a kid, intended or otherwise, resulted in being branded the worst. Pete had seen child molesters beaten senseless in jail. A man learned to endure the brunt of enmity from good citizens; from bad ones, it broached being lethal. In his wanderings from town to town, Pete cut a wide swath around anyone who might be a minor.

Smelling bad sometimes helped. Although kids stared with curiosity, they tended to avoid him. Adults did, too, but their stares were often accompanied by complaints to whoever was in charge. In Berrendo's library, Pete had heard many whispered conversations behind his back. Most of the librarians refused to recognize his existence except in those surreptitious discussions about the odious aspects of his presence, though there was one that treated him decent. She was slender with short auburn hair and soft gray eyes. He liked looking at her, and thought he had so far managed to do it without being noticed. Now that the weather was turning cold and he was planning to head for Florida, he wanted to find a way to thank her for her kindness.

He hadn't yet decided how to do that, but he knew her name and had found her address in the phone book. He had even followed her one of the times she walked home from work. As nearly as he could tell, she lived alone. So he figured, as long as he didn't make any move toward getting in, he could ring her doorbell and say what he wanted while she felt safe locked behind her screen. He didn't want to scare her, just find the words to express how grateful he felt to finally find someone capable of showing compassion without pity.

Rene Donnor was swallowing two Advils when the burly, lantern-jawed, blond man in the dark blue jacket walked through the door with a smug smile of self-assurance. She drained the last of the water from her paper cup, tossed it in the trash, and smiled back.

"I'm Detective Fuller from the B.P.D.," he said. "I need to talk to one of your students."

"Who's that?" she asked, wondering which of the brats was in trouble now.

"Nathan Wheeler."

Rene was surprised, knowing Nathan to be a well-behaved boy never before in any kind of trouble. "What's he done?"

"Nothing," the detective answered with a grin. "I just need to talk to him about a fight in the mall last night. Nathan saw what happened and might be able to help us out."

"Oh," she said with relief. But then, "I'm afraid all the students are at the pep rally just now. You'd be hard put to find any particular one till it's over."

He stared as if he hadn't understood, which she thought was a little dense for a detective.

"Come look," she said, beckoning him to join her at the window.

When they stood shoulder to shoulder staring through the glass, Buck saw the bleachers facing the football field crammed with students watching the cheerleaders go through their stunts. He would have liked to watch them himself but figured he better make a quick exit and come back later. Any time spent shooting the shit with the secretary was rich with opportunities to trip himself up. "When'll it be over?"

She looked at her watch, a tiny silver oval on her pale wrist. The cuff of her white sleeve was starched, the diamonds on her wedding ring sparkling as they caught sun. He became aware of her person, the compact shape of her butt under her green and blue plaid skirt below the green blazer, her breasts beneath the white blouse between her lapels, her gray hair shellacked in place, her lipstick a little off. Her eyes were slightly blurred, too, a symptom he pinned as the precursor of a migraine about to descend. He smiled at the thought that when he had come and gone again, her headache was sure to get a whole lot worse.

"I'm sorry," she apologized to what she saw in his smile. "The pep rally's just begun."

"I'll be back in an hour," he said, turning away before she saw anything else.

Rene watched him go, thinking the square cut of his shoulders were those of an exceptionally strong person. Not someone she cared to share space with, but then she didn't suppose being a police officer brought out the best in anyone. She returned to sit at her desk and close her eyes, grateful for a few more minutes of respite before the vice principal returned and she had to take the phones off hold and resume her duties.

The principal was in Socorro today, leaving Mr. Barrow in charge. Rene didn't care for the vice principal. He was only thirty-two and effete in her estimation, while she was forty-five and considered herself stalwart. She wondered if working so closely with him had brought on her headache. Bill Shane was more of a disciplinarian, while Tom Barrow was very much too lenient, especially with girls. When Amy Sterling came in with that message from Mrs. Blair, Mr. Shane would have taken one look at the girl's blouse with its décolletage worthy of a harlot and sent her home on the spot. Tom Barrow hadn't even noticed the girl's attire was hardly in keeping with the school's dress code. Even Amy seemed disappointed with his lack of astuteness, which made Rene suspect the girl's intention had been to test Mr. Shane's tolerance.

Rene supposed that wasn't surprising since Amy came from a single-parent home, that designation almost always meaning only a mother. Girls without fathers tended to be promiscuous, in Rene's opinion. Of course boys without fathers were no better. Both of them challenged authority in ways that children who grew up under a man's discipline didn't. Nathan Wheeler was the exception to that. Everyone knew his parents had all but abandoned him, but he had taken the change in stride, adjusting to living in a foster home as if there was no difference. Perhaps there wasn't, Rene decided. Because parents are physically present didn't necessarily mean they were involved in their children's lives.

She wondered what it was that Nathan had witnessed at the mall. Thursday wasn't typically the night for kids to act up. She hadn't heard about a fight, but she didn't suppose there was any reason she would have short of someone being murdered, which was almost unknown in Berrendo. When it did happen, it was usually those Mexicans. Hispanics, they were called now. They had a violent culture, due no doubt to being Catholic and receiving forgiveness in confession for everything they did.

Rene laid her head on her folded arms on her desk. The pain was worse now. She must stop thinking. Lord knows she couldn't solve the world's problems by sitting alone in an office and cogitating herself into misery. She had to concentrate on calming thoughts, visualize peaceful scenes. Her grandson's third birthday party last weekend had been such fun. His sweet little face above the candles! Maybe she should retire and work in the church's daycare. One didn't have to think with infants. Didn't have to explain the rules or make decisions more difficult than when to change their diapers.

That was the problem! Mr. Barrow expected her to make too many of the decisions Mr. Shane always made. She was only the school secretary, after all. Even if she *had* been here ten years and this was Mr. Barrow's first, he was her superior, the responsibility was his. Those words became a litany she repeated like a mantra, allowing her to fall briefly asleep. Waking a few minutes later, her headache diminished to a manageable pain, Rene reapplied her lipstick so her smile would be bright when the detective returned.

Chapter Two

Buck drove past the miniature golf course on his right, past the bowling alley on his left, and kept going until he saw the back entrance to the cemetery across from the county fairgrounds. Coasting under the dappled shade of evergreens planted to commemorate the dead, he listened to the finely ground gravel crunch under his tires as he searched the deeper shadows for his cousin.

Peering unhappily at the slow-moving station wagon, Zeb was sitting on one of the crypts built above ground, his red polo shirt and jet-black slacks so spiffy he could have passed for a military cadet. As Buck drifted to a stop in the sunny lane and cut the engine, they watched each other, both waiting for the other to make the first move. Finally Buck opened his door and stepped out, though he stayed by the car, hesitant to join his cousin on a tomb.

Zeb stood up and ambled closer. His topaz eyes—cat's eyes is how Buck always thought of them—searched the back of the car, then met Buck's with a silent demand for an explanation.

Buck laughed. "They were having some kinda pep rally and the secretary wouldn't get him out. I'll go back in a bit, no sweat."

But he *was* sweating, standing there in the sun wearing a dark jacket that soaked in heat. He would have taken the jacket off and tossed it in the car except he didn't want it wrinkled until this charade was over. Watching Zeb turn his back to stare out at the traffic on Southeast Main, Buck listened to the ticking of the Pontiac's engine, as the turn signal had ticked earlier, counting off the minutes Nathan Wheeler had left free of pain.

Zeb turned around and jerked his head to throw his forelock out of his eyes, his dark hair almost black, his eyes that weird topaz Buck found creepy. "You sure it wasn't a stall?"

Buck shrugged. "The bitch took me to the window and showed me all the kids on the bleachers. Short of making an announcement over the loudspeaker, there wasn't no way to find any one in particular."

"Thought you were going to get him out of first period."

"I was late."

"Why?"

Buck remembered not wanting to walk past the cop in Denny's. "I ran into an acquaintance wanted to shoot the shit. Would've looked funny if I cut him off."

"Who was it?" Zeb asked, quick as a bullet.

"Just a guy from up north. You don't know him."

"What's his name?"

"Tom, Dick, I don't know. What's it matter?"

"What'd you tell him about where you were going all dressed up?"

"I ain't dressed up 'cause I'm wearing a coat and tie. Lotsa men wear 'em all the time."

"You don't."

Buck shrugged. "I told him I had a job as a salesman. Was waiting on an appointment."

"What're you selling?"

"What is this? Twenty questions? I shot the shit and left. There's no problem, Zeb."

"Then why're you sweating?"

Buck reached through the open driver's door and picked up the motel towel he'd brought in case something needed wiping off. Mopping his face and neck, he grinned at his cousin, then tossed the towel on the backseat floor. "It's fucking hot, in case you ain't noticed."

But Zeb wasn't sweating, standing there in his knit shirt and black pants. Course Zeb didn't have to do nothing but wait in the shade. Buck was taking all the risk, here at the start. If Zeb didn't sweat later, Buck would suspect his cousin was a zombie, but all he said was, "Wish you'd gotten me a better car."

"That Pontiac cost me eight hundred dollars. How much money you think I have laying around?"

Buck hadn't seen eight hundred dollars all together since he robbed that convenience store a couple years back. "Thought you'd get me one I'd wanta keep."

"You want to be caught driving around in the get-away car?"

"Be nice to have some kinda vehicle."

"You do this job right, I'll set you up with something in the family business."

"That sounds good, Zeb, but ain't you gonna go to college 'fore you start working for your granddad?"

Zeb shook his head. "I'm going to stay here and marry Amy."

"That's big of you after what was done to her."

Zeb's smile was sleazy with triumph, as if he'd gain good time in heaven for having married damaged goods. Buck looked at his watch. "Guess I oughta get back."

"Guess you oughta."

"Wanted to let you know why I was late."

"Appreciate it."

Buck shivered in the sun. "You all right here?"

"Yeah, I like graveyards. When you come back, bring me a Coke."

"Have to pick it up 'fore I get the kid."

"Don't get me one in a can. Go to McDonalds and ask for extra ice."

"Okay," Buck said, almost smiling to know Zeb was feeling the heat after all.

Nathan Wheeler stood with his rifle at ground rest while he searched the packed bleachers for Amy. He found her way high up with her friend Nora. Seeing Amy wave, he wished he could wave back but he was supposed to stand at attention until ordered to escort the colors off the field. He was already hot in the sun, his wool uniform prickly with sweat, and he felt impatient to finish his duty and find Amy again, hoping she would say something about how handsome he looked.

Now that he had made up his mind to propose, he wasn't sure he could wait another day. Maybe he would ask her tonight after the game, though they weren't going there together because Amy's mother wouldn't let them date more than once in a weekend. They circumvented that by going the same places separately. Tonight the Berrendo Coyotes were playing the Carlsbad Cavemen. Everyone was already excited. If the Coyotes won, the happiness would float a combat tank. Even if they lost, the expended energy would leave a lull of melancholy fit to be filled by something as sweet as a proposal of marriage.

If she turned him down tonight, however, he wasn't sure he could face her again on Saturday, which would make for a miserable weekend. Maybe it was better to wait, not just for Saturday but for Christmas, or their first anniversary, any distant date that would postpone the emptiness he would feel knowing she wouldn't marry him. He closed his eyes and let that loneliness sweep over him. The band's clumsy rendition of the national anthem diminished into a whisper softer than the pulse in his ears, the flood of blood through his veins. Isolated behind the red filigree of his eyelids, he was momentarily alone, not physically as he was without parents, or spiritually as in his newly assumed stance of agnosticism, but existentially conscious of every man's utter solitude. He opened his eyes and saw the bleachers again, Amy's face among the collage of eyes and mouths beneath windblown wreaths and tendrils of hair. In that clear moment of insight, he knew his life would be empty from the moment Amy refused him, and that his awful need could make him hesitate too long.

He responded to the sergeant's command and raised his rifle to present the colors, heard the flag snap in the wind, then the slap of his hand on the wooden stock, the metallic click of the bolt action. The blue sky was brazen in his eyes as he fired a blank into oblivion, the shade beneath the visor of his cap comforting as he slung the rifle across his shoulder and marched off the field knowing that, because of the existential moment just passed, he had already left childhood behind and advanced into his first moment of manhood.

In the crowd afterward, he found Amy as easily as if they were connected by an invisible string. Unable to hug beneath the censuring gaze of the teachers, they held hands between their parallel thighs as Nora chattered on about something the coach had said during the rally. Nathan looked into Amy's eyes and saw his future in their shine of admiration at the figure he cut in his uniform, so hot in the sun. Then he adjusted his glasses on his nose, slippery with sweat, and tried to concentrate on what Nora was saying.

★ ★ ★ ★ ★

Buck checked himself in the rearview mirror and picked a shred of hamburger lettuce out of his teeth before opening the car door. He practiced an officious looking smile as he crossed the grass between the visitors' parking and the school. Once inside he didn't hesitate, knowing a real cop wouldn't, and besides, he knew where he was going.

Both ends of the hall were closed with glass doors streaming with sunshine that made the corridor a tunnel of light reflecting off the shiny green floor and glossy white walls. He had been waiting his whole life for this. All the moments of terror and shame, some of which had happened in halls very similar to these, had been a gauntlet earning him this chance to seal his future as Zeb Mulroney's right-hand man. Buck would have whistled if he had ever learned how, but it was enough that he was humming inside his head. The tune was a happy one because if there was one thing he knew, it was that self-fulfilling prophecies always came true. That's what he considered himself, a prophecy of merit about to be rewarded.

He chuckled when he opened the door, then restrained his amusement as the secretary looked up without any apparent alarm to see disaster in the form of Buck Powell saunter into her arena.

"Pep rally over?" he asked in a jovial tone.

"I'll buzz Mr. Barrow," she said, reaching for the phone. "He's in charge today, though he's only the vice principal." She waited with the phone pressed to her ear.

Buck raised his eyebrows and nodded with a smile, impressed with his luck that the chief honcho was out of town. He had to restrain his grin when he heard the secretary say, "That police detective is here again, Mr. Barrow."

Almost immediately the door bearing his nameplate

opened and Tom Barrow came out, extending his hand with an aura of being willing to please.

"Detective John Fuller," Buck lied, shaking the vice principal's hand. "I need to take Nathan Wheeler downtown for questioning."

"Is he in trouble?" Barrow asked, obviously already having heard the answer from the secretary.

Buck shook his head. "Witnessed a fight in the mall last night. Was some pretty heavy damage done to one of the storefronts and we got a lineup ready to go. Wanta see if Nathan can I.D. any of our suspects."

Barrow turned to Mrs. Donnor—Buck knew her name by the plate on the front of her desk—and said, "Will you run down and get him?"

"Surely," she said, rising gracefully.

Again Buck had to stop himself from grinning, thinking these folks were so cooperative they had already figured out where the kid was, which classroom and all. He was half-surprised they didn't have Nathan sitting in one of those wooden chairs lined up against the wall. "Big game tonight, huh?"

Tom Barrow nodded. "Guess you're not from Berrendo."

Buck tried to make his voice drawl when he said, "No, I came over from Odessa just last year."

Barrow nodded again. "The game tonight's against the Carlsbad Cavemen, our traditional rivals."

"Ever been to Yuma, Arizona?"

"I've been through there."

"Know the name of their high school team?"

Barrow shook his head.

"The Criminals, on account of that old prison they got."

Barrow winced. "That's about the worst name for a school team I've ever heard."

"Makes you wonder, don't it," Buck agreed.

They both turned to face the door, hearing the tap of high heels accompanied by softer footsteps in the hall.

Nathan looked curious, no more than that, as he entered the office. He scrutinized Buck, then shifted his gaze to the vice principal and waited for an explanation. The secretary walked behind her desk and sat down.

"Nathan," Barrow said softly, "this is Detective John Fuller from the police department."

Nathan's eyes narrowed behind his black horn-rimmed glasses as he looked at Buck.

"Just taking you to the station for a few questions," Buck said.

Mrs. Donnor said, "Should we call his home and let them know what's happening?"

Buck forced himself to smile though he wanted to hit the bitch. "I'd appreciate it if you'd do that, ma'am. Tell 'em they can pick him up in an hour or so."

"Surely," she said, giving Nathan a cheerful smile.

Barrow said, "This is no big deal, Nathan. You might even find it fun." He winked at Buck.

Buck almost laughed, thinking one thing he could guarantee was that Nathan would find no fun in what lay ahead. "Let's go," he told the kid, who still looked confused. But he came along easily enough. Cowed by authority, Buck thought. That's what's wrong with the younger generation. Do what they're told entirely too easily, though in this case he was glad.

In the parking lot, he led the kid to the Pontiac and told him to put both hands on the front fender and spread his legs. Nathan did it, throwing a quizzical look over his shoulder.

"Just gonna frisk ya, kid," Buck said. "Regulations, is all."

He ran his hands along the boy's body, front and back,

arms and legs, while the boy said in a bewildered tone, "I don't have any weapons."

"No, you don't," Buck agreed. "You can stand up now." He pulled the handcuffs out of his jacket pocket. "Put your hands behind your back."

"Is this necessary?" Nathan asked, the disdain in his voice hinting at a resurgence of courage.

But it was too late. "Regulations," Buck said again. After snapping the cuffs on, he opened the back door and gestured for the kid to get in.

Nathan hesitated, seeing the small towel and a length of rope on the floor, ordinary things in an ordinary car.

"You can step on those," Buck said. "You won't hurt nothing."

But Nathan was a good kid, mindful of others' possessions. He turned around and sat on the seat before swiveling his legs in. Even then, he swung his feet over and set them down on the far side.

Buck let himself grin as he slammed the door locked and got in behind the wheel. Backing out of the parking space, he glanced at the kid a few times, but Nathan was looking at the school as if thinking of something he had left behind. Buck wanted to tell the kid to forget whatever it was, that nothing was more important than what was about to come down, but he kept quiet as he left the lot and turned west on Hobbs.

Tom Barrow stood at his office window, a nudge of doubt souring his stomach as he watched the burly detective frisk and handcuff Nathan Wheeler. Tom hadn't expected the boy to be handcuffed. After all, he hadn't done anything wrong, merely witnessed a fight at the mall, at least that's what the detective had said. So why the handcuffs? And then when he opened the back door and the boy got in, Tom saw trash on the floor. He didn't suppose there was any reason why a policeman wouldn't have trash on the floor of his car like anyone else, but Tom couldn't deny his suspicion that something was wrong. Maybe it was the car. The old green Pontiac somehow didn't seem right. For one thing, Tom had never seen a cop, even an undercover one, drive a car with out-of-state plates.

Sweat swamped his armpits when he realized he hadn't asked to see any identification. He started toward the outer office to ask Mrs. Donnor if she had seen any, then stopped, his neck clammy beneath the collar of his shirt. If she hadn't, and he hadn't, what then? He closed his eyes, meeting in his mind the eyes of Nathan Wheeler looking back at the school as he was being driven away.

Tom sat down heavily behind his desk, staring at the open door as he argued with himself that the boy hadn't put up any resistance. Would Nathan go along like that if he hadn't witnessed a fight at the mall? But did anyone tell him why he was being taken out of school? Tom thought hard. All he could remember was the detective telling Nathan he wanted to ask him some questions at the station. Then Mrs. Donnor had asked if she should call Nathan's home and tell his foster mother what was happening.

Tom remembered the detective had flinched when she made that suggestion. Though the detective had hidden it behind a quick smile, Tom couldn't deny having seen it. Arguing with himself that no one would kidnap Nathan Wheeler, a poor boy living in a foster home, Tom was unable to shake his growing conviction that the man who took Nathan out of school was in no way connected to any police force. Now Tom felt sick. Not only hadn't he asked for identification, he had forgotten the man's name. Forcing himself to his feet, he walked to the door and stood looking out at Mrs.

Donnor where she sat behind her desk. He cleared his throat, as much for his own sake as to attract her attention. She looked up, her face unfriendly. He had known since the first day of school that she didn't like him, but this went way beyond petty rifts between personalities. "Rene," he said, then had to start over because his voice barely made it past the constriction in his throat. "Rene, do you remember the name the detective gave us?"

"Of the boy he wanted?" she asked as if Tom were a fool. "Nathan Wheeler is who he asked for, and that's who he got."

"No, his name," Tom said. "The detective's."

"John Fuller."

"When he first came this morning, did you see his badge?"

Her face lost color behind the mask of her makeup. "Didn't you see it?"

"I assumed you had."

After a moment, she whispered, "Dear God."

"You've lived here all your life," Tom said, trying not to sound accusing. "Don't you know the men on the police force?"

"There's fifty thousand people in Berrendo! I can't know them all!"

"No, of course not," Tom said. "I'm sure it'll be okay. I mean, there's no doubt we should have checked the man's I.D., but I can't think of any reason why an unwarranted person would take Nathan Wheeler out of school. Can you?"

She shook her head, but he saw judgment in her eyes. It had been his responsibility. He was in charge.

"As long as there're no further developments," he pleaded, "can we keep this between ourselves?"

"I don't know," she answered. "We'll have to see what happens, won't we."

He nodded and returned to his office, knowing she would not keep it to herself, and that, as of now, his future in education was doubtful at best.

Buck glanced at the kid in the mirror, seeing he had caught on that the way they were going wouldn't take them anywhere near the police station.

"Got one more stop to make," Buck said to stall the kid's worry.

Nathan looked out the window without saying anything.

Buck turned south on Sunset. He had his window down, his elbow on the edge, and was feeling confident right then. It had all gone so smooth, he figured the next step would be just as easy. When he leaned forward and took the paper bag off the floor on the passenger side, the kid didn't even react. Out of the bag Buck shook a washcloth and can of engine starter, and still Nathan just sat staring out the window, obviously unhappy but not alarmed.

Buck slowed down as he approached Sunset Park. Nathan perked up a little, watching straight ahead as Buck pulled onto the dirt road defining the park's perimeter. He stopped the Pontiac behind the baseball diamond and shut off the engine. Nathan was looking around now, seeing no one else. Buck picked up the can of starter in his right hand and the cloth in his left, sprayed a thick layer of fluid, saturating the cloth with ether, then dropped the can, swiveled around to lean over the seat, grab the back of the kid's head, and jam the cloth against his face before Nathan could identify what he was smelling.

He fought for a few seconds, but there was so much ether in the cloth that Buck was dizzy before the kid slumped limp. Buck threw the cloth out the window, then stayed leaning over the back of the front seat, breathing fast while he watched the kid, who had fallen sideways on the seat and wasn't moving. Buck leaned farther down to reach the rope. He rolled Nathan onto the floor, made a quick hogtie around the kid's ankles, and tied them to the chain connecting the handcuffs. Sweating hard, he jabbed himself behind the wheel, started the engine, and drove quickly out of the park and into the south flow of traffic on Sunset. After a while his breathing returned to normal and he wasn't sweating so much, though he wished he had the towel that was now under the kid's feet. But he left the window open and the breeze eventually did what any towel could.

When he came to a stretch where he had the road to himself, he tossed the can of starter fluid over the Pontiac's roof into clumps of purple prickly clover. He drove farther south than he had to. Congratulating himself on having pulled it off, he grinned into the rearview mirror and saw a squad car in the lane behind him. He let off on the accelerator at the same time that he glanced at the speedometer. He was only doing thirty-five and didn't figure the limit could be much less. Staring straight ahead, he tried to act calm, knowing cops could smell fear. Something in sweat changed when people were scared, sending out an odor only certain others were capable of picking up, like that guy at the diner this morning. Buck kept glancing into the rearview, trying not to will the cop to leave him alone, afraid even a silent negative would be caught. Finally the cop turned left on Poe.

Buck continued south on Sunset until it turned into the Y/O Ranch Road and he was so far out he saw antelope on the prairie. He almost stopped and dumped the kid, figuring he could sell the car in El Paso and blow his cousin off when Zeb came around demanding an explanation. That cop had scared Buck, reviving strong prison memories, and suddenly he wasn't sure he wanted to go through with whatever Zeb had planned. He made a couple of turns on the back country roads until he found himself almost into the mountains before he came to his senses. Zeb was gonna be pissed if he didn't get to that cemetery damn quick. What was he thinking, double-crossing the only chance at a meal ticket he was likely to get? By the time he turned east on Brasher, he was feeling cocky again. The ether smell was gone and there wasn't a peep from the kid. Cousin Zeb was gonna be pleased.

Chapter Three

On her belly in bed, Lucinda was enjoying the rhythm of Devon's palm gently caressing her bottom. After having made love with the leisure of knowing they still had hours of solitude ahead, she was savoring his caresses until he spoiled her pleasure by saying, "For an old lady, you've got a beautiful ass."

She rolled over to face him, her expression evidently one of consternation because he said apologetically, "I was kidding."

"How old do you think I am?"

"Forty-one. I've seen your driver's license, remember?"

"You picked it up off the floor. I didn't know you'd read it." He shrugged.

"How old are you?" she asked, catching a note of accusation in her voice.

"Thirty-five."

She looked away.

"Not such a difference," he said gently.

"Depends on who's calling it," she muttered.

He lay down close beside her. Aware of the contours of their bodies pressed so comfortably together, she asked, "What are we, Devon? Just a landlady and tenant who've found an unexpected bonus in our business arrangement?" His silence wasn't unpleasant, which encouraged her to continue. "Friends who're lucky enough to enjoy sex without repercussions?"

"That sounds good."

"Not romantically involved?"

"Is that what you want?"

She shrugged, then met his eyes and shook her head. "I'm happy with the way things are."

"Why are we having this conversation then?"

Her smile felt weak. "I thought maybe we could go out sometime but, you know," she paused to shrug again, staring at the ceiling, "it's a small town and we'll no doubt be seen."

"No doubt," he teased.

She met his eyes.

He smiled. "Why don't I take you and Amy to the football game tonight? That'll look innocent enough."

She laughed. "If I can keep my hands to myself."

"That's up to you. I don't have anything to lose."

She nodded, aware of his point, which she guessed was why she had made them both uncomfortable by bringing this up in the first place. "Did you know tonight's game is in Carlsbad?"

"Yes, and I'll make the drive if you don't mind traveling that far in my truck."

"I like your truck." She sighed. "I wish we could spend the night together sometime."

"We could, if Amy would stay over with a girlfriend."

"Yes, but she'd have to come up with the idea. I can't banish her from the house."

"Would you be okay with leaving her alone?"

"Yeah, sure. I mean, she's seventeen."

"We could spend a weekend in the mountains. Rent a cabin, go for walks in the woods." He traced his fingertips along the inside of her thigh. "Make love in front of a fire."

"Sounds nice."

"Want me to make reservations for next weekend?"

"Use my phone," she said. "I can pay for that much."

He pulled on his jeans and walked into the kitchen. Listening to him take the phonebook out of the drawer, then punch in a number, she rolled over to look at the bedside alarm. One o'clock. They had two hours yet. Unless the school closed early again. Remembering last Friday afternoon, she suspected Amy had seen her in Devon's bed. Careless of them not to close the shutters, but it hadn't occurred to Lucinda that her daughter might come home early because of a bomb threat. They didn't have such things when she went to school. Listening to his voice from the kitchen, she wondered if maybe his being a police officer wasn't why she had fallen in love so quickly, as if being a cop meant he could protect them from the violence now rife in the world. Ex-cop, she reminded herself. And there was that, too: maybe whatever had motivated him to quit wasn't as benign as she preferred to assume. She decided that as soon as she was alone, she would call the police in El Paso and find out whatever they were willing to tell her about why he was no longer among them.

Knowing how easily he could no longer be among her and Amy, she closed her eyes and concentrated on the inflections in his voice as he spoke on the phone. She did love having him in her life. Yet she knew she had been remiss in not checking his references before bringing him into the small home she shared with her nearly-grown daughter. Suppressing a wave of guilt, she opened her eyes and saw him standing barechested in her doorway, a vision she had given up on ever owning again: a handsome man admiring her in bed.

Pete Reck made himself as presentable as possible in the men's room at the library. He slicked back his wet hair and rinsed out his mouth, not wanting to offend the librarian with bad breath on top of a ripe case of b.o. Considering his appearance in the mirror, he decided he could pass for presentable. His black hair looked neat, his beard was free of debris, there weren't any crusts around his glittering dark eyes, and with his jacket buttoned no one could see the bloodstains on his shirt, souvenirs of an unfriendly encounter last night in the park.

He had found an unopened package of hot dogs in the Dumpster behind a grocery store. The expiration date was only a week old, so he figured, with all the preservatives in processed meat, it was safe. To go with his main course, he found a squashed tin of chocolate pudding still intact. From a deli's sidewalk table he took little envelopes of mustard and a handful of Sweet 'N Low. The latter he poured in an old paper cup filled with water, then he sat under a tree by the North Spring River and finished his feast in the company of grackles, the shiny black birds whistling like magpies. Afterwards, he fell asleep. When he woke up, he was surrounded by punks laughing as they watched him cornered against the tree.

In the wake of the fight he had lost his supper and gained a bloody nose, but he wasn't bruised any place visible in the mirror of the library's restroom. Though his ribs felt sore and his knuckles were scabbed, he planned on keeping his hands in his pockets and definitely didn't anticipate unbuttoning his jacket, let alone taking off his shirt. He shouldered his khaki backpack with his sleeping bag tied to the bottom, then walked into the lobby and looked past the checkout counter to the reference desk. Seeing another woman was there, the short one with curly gray hair and half-glasses riding the end of her nose, he hesitated before forcing himself forward, watching for the exact moment she became aware of his approach.

Her nostrils flared as she looked up, alarm snapping like

pennants in her pale blue eyes. When he was in front of her desk, he scrunched down a little, making her lean back in her chair so he had to get even closer to speak as softly as he wanted.

" 'Cuse me," he said.

She slowly blinked, her upturned nose saying she wouldn't excuse him for anything as long as he smelled the way he did.

Her scent was from the dozen different products she sprayed and fluffed on herself, an amalgam of synthetic fragrances sufficiently incompatible to make him sneeze. "I was wondering," he said in a near whisper, "if I could talk to the other lady."

"Who?" she asked, sounding like an owl.

"The one here earlier," he mumbled.

"I don't know who was here before I arrived."

He figured she probably did know, that they had some kind of schedule tacked on a wall somewhere, but he kept his voice soft when he said, "Lucinda Sterling's the name on her tag."

The gray-haired lady covered her own tag in an unconscious gesture of concealment. "She left already."

He glanced at the clock. "You mean for lunch?"

The lady shook her head. "She only works half-days on Fridays."

Muttering a curse, he wondered if this obstacle meant he shouldn't try to thank Lucinda Sterling, that it wasn't destined to happen.

In a wheedling tone, the lady said, "You can come back tomorrow, can't you?"

She looked so intimidated he felt tempted to flap his arms and caw like a crow. But the one time he had given in to such an inclination, he had ended up in jail. That happened in Tucson, a city accustomed to transients and unwilling to cut them slack. So far the police in Berrendo had been lenient, and he didn't care to tempt fate. Though he couldn't bring himself to thank the lady for treating him like vermin, he managed to nod before turning away. All the way out the door he could feel her wishing him good riddance.

It was still the lunch hour and he didn't think he could show up in Lucinda's neighborhood at this time of day. Someone would see him and call the cops. Maybe a little later in the afternoon, when the old folks would be napping, the guardians who sat in the sun on front porches noting every sliver of change in a landscape they oversaw daily as their major activity. They wouldn't all be asleep, someone would see him, but the lethargy of late afternoon might allow him to come and go without being molested; at least he'd have a better chance than now.

Zeb Mulroney lay on the cool granite crypt and watched the evergreen needles bounce overhead in the wind. The needles made a crinkly sound because the trees were dry in the dregs of September, as dry as his mouth as he waited for the Coke his cousin would bring. Not having been surprised to see Buck last time with an empty car, Zeb would be even less surprised if the only thing he brought this time was the Coke, probably in a can from a store, or at best a cup without enough ice so what was there had already melted. Buck's life up to this point wasn't a paradigm of success, so Zeb figured hoping for results was like expecting a miracle. He had been astonished when the buffoon not only went along with the plan, but agreed to take the initial risk. Once it was over, only his word could implicate Zeb. And who would believe an unemployed ex-con over the scion of the wealthiest family in this corner of the state? Nobody, Zeb was counting on that.

Last week, when his mother had asked him to pick up his

cousin at the Albuquerque airport, Zeb had agreed with no ulterior motive. It was when they were driving home that the plan had unfolded. Buck was tall and stout, blond and affable behind the wheel of the new red Spyder, while dark, wiry Zeb felt like a hornet whining in the black leather passenger seat. He had wanted to get high but Buck didn't have any drugs, so they settled for nipping at a bottle of Chivas as they sped through the hills studded with scrubby piñon, heading toward the oil-rich prairie that was home to the Mulroneys and, farther south, the Powells, descendants of Zeb's great aunt and uncle who stuck with cattle and went broke in the drought preceding the Depression.

Buck was twenty-five and Zeb eighteen, but it was Zeb's car Buck was driving and Zeb's money he had spent in the liquor store in Albuquerque and then again when they bought lunch in Vaughn. Zeb wore clothes from exclusive shops in Phoenix and Dallas while Buck's style came from Wal-Mart, and Zeb's sneakers cost more than Buck had to his name. But Buck was accustomed to cheerfully dodging the vagaries of life in his scuffed, cloned Ropers while Zeb skulked through his days in hundred-dollar sneakers.

Zeb took another sip of scotch, corked the bottle and set it on the floor between his feet, then looked out at a jagged red arroyo slashing the land. "There's a twerp in school's been giving me grief," he said, not expecting anything to come of his chance remark. When he looked over at his cousin, however, Buck actually seemed concerned, which made Zeb laugh. "Are you thinking you could maybe do something about it?"

"Depends on what kinda grief," Buck answered with an ingratiating smile.

"Girl kind."

"Somebody took a girl from you?" Buck asked incredulously.

Unable to bring himself to admit that, Zeb shook his head. "Worse."

Buck waited.

"She wasn't exactly my girl," Zeb explained, concocting his tale as he went. "I'd dated her a coupla times, but she was the kind you treat with respect, know what I mean?"

Buck nodded, meeting Zeb's eyes. Before looking back at the road, he glanced at the bottle, but Zeb left it on the floor. "What's her name?" Buck asked.

"Amy Sterling," Zeb said.

"What's she look like?"

"Big blue eyes and long black hair. That's a dynamite combination, don't you think?"

Buck nodded. "Nice otherwise, too?"

Zeb decided to titillate his cousin. "Amy's not as skinny as a lot of girls. She's got some flesh to grab onto." He laughed. "Tits to hell and gone. Little waist, tight ass, long legs. Dynamite, like I said."

Buck nodded again, his eyes bright.

"This dude," Zeb continued, "is slime. I've seen how he tricks girls to get what he wants, then ignores them so they're crying as they watch him walk by." He smiled, remembering those sad faces and how the hurt in them always made him hot. But that wasn't the story he was telling.

"Is that what he did to Amy?"

"Worse. He raped her. Last Friday night."

"Did she blow the whistle?"

Zeb shook his head. "Too embarrassed."

"So how d'ya know it happened?"

"It's all over school. And this dude, he's strutting his stuff. It's disgusting."

"What's his name?"

"Nathan Wheeler. I'd like to take him down."

A mile went by with neither of them speaking, a mile in which the hills diminished into grassland prairie, flat and brown after the first freeze of autumn; a minute in which Zeb's pulse kept steady at eighty but Buck's peaked at ninety-two.

"So do you think you could help me out?"

"What'd you have in mind?"

"Payback." Zeb laughed. "Fuck the fucker."

"Sodomy?"

Zeb appraised him with more appreciation. "Did you do that in prison?"

Buck shook his head.

"Was it the other way around?"

"No, but I heard a lot of it coming down."

"You mean like the guy was screaming?"

Buck nodded.

"Wow."

"I won't do nothing like that."

"What about beating the shit out of him? Would you do that?"

Buck looked at the prairie stretching empty all around. "How've you got it figured?"

It was dark when they reached Berrendo. Buck had meant to catch a bus south to Artesia if his cousin wouldn't drive him that far, but he was amenable to letting Zeb put him up in a motel until the job was done. Buck would have chosen a nicer motel, but Zeb said he didn't have much cash, and since they had to buy a car for the caper, he had to go cheap. Still in all, it was a room not unlike the ones Buck was used to, and it was free.

The next day he crossed the street to the Circle K to get some food. Wandering the aisles, he counted in his head the money he had and what he thought he might spend without leaving himself too short. He had been standing in the automotive section for a few minutes before he realized why he was there. At first it was a mystery since the shelves held nothing edible, but then his gaze focused on half a dozen cans of engine starter. He read the ingredients on the two different brands and chose the one containing the most ether, then he bought a box of glazed doughnuts, a sausage and egg sandwich he microwaved hot, and a cold six-pack of Dr Pepper. All told his purchases amounted to $13.47. He kept the receipt in case Zeb offered to reimburse him.

Back in the motel room, he put the food on the night stand and set the starter fluid on top of the TV so he could see it while he ate. The starter perched there made him feel smart.

By noon, he had eaten all his food and felt bored watching cartoons in the crummy room. He walked north to Little Caesar's. At the counter he ordered a large pepperoni and a big cup of Coke, then sat at a table by the window to wait. Beyond the sparsely filled parking lot, a steady flow of traffic zipped up and down Main, and he made a game of trying to pick Nathan Wheeler out of the passengers inside the cars. It wasn't until he had gone back to the counter to pick up his pizza that he realized Nathan, like Zeb, would be in school, not out driving around. Again at his table by the window, he shrugged it off, thinking the game had been fun and probably not any more meaningless than the rest of his life.

Finding himself out of Coke before his pizza was half-gone, he carried his cup over to the dispenser and stood in line behind a fat woman helping a toddler draw her own drink. He smiled at the woman as she grabbed the kid out of his way. She didn't return the smile, which made him wonder if he smelled bad. As he sat down to finish his pizza, he decided to take a shower when he returned to his room. Before going back, he went into the Dollar Daze next door and spent six bucks on a blue T-shirt only one size too small.

He'd had his shower and was wearing the shirt and a clean pair of jeans while watching a re-run of *The Brady Bunch* when Zeb walked in with a plastic bag of purchases he dumped out on the bed. Buck stared at the stark display against the grainy gray sheet: an ice pick, a pair of rubber-grip pliers, and two steak knives packaged on one shrink-wrapped piece of cardboard. The sharp metal edges made him realize how serious Zeb was, which made him even more proud to point out the can of starter fluid. When Zeb picked it up and read that it contained mostly ether, his smile was unlike any Buck had seen since being cut loose from prison. That kind of smile carried a warmth well known in the tight circles of criminal conspiracy, and Buck felt happy to share one again.

In the long shadows of the escaping afternoon, Zeb drove Buck around town in his Spyder. When Buck spotted a pawnshop on West 2nd, he asked Zeb to stop. Buck went in alone and shared more of that same kind of smile with the man behind the counter as he made his selections. Coming out with his small paper bag, he grinned at Zeb, raising the ante of the smiles in proportion to what was being invested. Inside the car, he opened the bag and let Zeb see a set of gleaming stainless steel handcuffs.

Zeb laughed, starting the engine and shifting into reverse. "This is cool," he chortled, nearly beside himself with glee.

Buck felt so proud to please his Cousin Zeb that he was able to keep secret his more important purchase: a snubbed .38 pressed against his left ankle inside his boot. He figured, when they got into the kind of pinch only a gun can get a man out of, that's when he'd pull the .38 and cinch his reputation as a man worth his weight.

Whispering inside the motel room, they made their final

plans, then Zeb left Buck alone, promising to return with a get-away car nobody local would recognize. The sight of the Pontiac was Buck's first disappointment with Zeb. Learning there wasn't any money for reimbursement was his second. But believing Zeb would come through in the end, he went to sleep that night confident the next day would see the dawning of his abundant and commodious future.

Zeb felt equally confident. For a long time he had believed if he could vent his wrath in one conflagration of violence, he would expel his need and be able to settle into the comfortable amiability that seemed normal in everyone else. Nathan Wheeler presented a perfect target, protecting the colors in his Dudley Do-Right uniform while carrying a rifle everyone knew was a sham. Zeb carried a gun, often to class, but it wasn't a prop and he didn't flaunt it, knowing the principal would not only confiscate the weapon but suspend him, too. Zeb couldn't afford to miss any more school unless he wanted to go another year to graduate, which he didn't. He'd had enough of grownups pushing him around.

In addition to his impotent gun, Nathan had a quiet quality Zeb found obnoxious, as if he didn't need to assert his rights to attract anyone's attention. He just smugly went about his business, getting such good grades he raised the curve for everyone else, saying "Yes, ma'am" and "No, sir" so the teachers fawned over him, and generally acting fucking happy when everyone knew he lived in a foster home because his parents couldn't be bothered. On top of all that, he was dating Amy Sterling, the only girl in school Zeb wanted. There were plenty of girls who would put out, and he made use of their weakness, but it was Amy's submission he craved.

Last year they had dated for several months, and Zeb had thought he was getting close to scoring when all of a sudden she quit seeing him. He had planned his seduction as carefully as anything he'd ever done, granting all her wishes and conceding to all her conditions. Then one time, one fucking time, he went ballistic and kicked Joe Mason in the balls 'cause Joe lost their money on a drug deal he had promised would come down with no hitch.

Looking terrified, Amy had backed away from Zeb and wouldn't let him drive her home. She called her mother and waited in the lobby of the theater until Mrs. Sterling's car was at the curb. Even then, she ran the scant distance to the open car door, and Mrs. Sterling stepped on the gas as if Zeb were a vampire out to suck Amy's blood. He would have chased her except he had to deal with the cops. Someone had called them, along with an ambulance, when Joe couldn't get up. Being who he was, Zeb hadn't been arrested, but he had been powerless to stop Amy from leaving without him.

His father was drunk when Zeb got home. His speech slurred, Silas shouted that the chief of police had called to tell him what had happened and warn him again that Little Zeb was out of control. All the frustrations and disappointments of the old man's pathetic life were focused on Zeb the minute he walked through the door. After the initial outburst, neither of them spoke, their mutual hatred rankling between them. Then Silas had picked up a vase and thrown it at Zeb, who watched it come, thinking the depth of his father's intoxication decreed failure. Coming to, naked in bed, his wrists shackled to the headboard, he realized he had been wrong. Silas stood nearby, a belt in one hand, in the other a drink he had finished while waiting for Zeb to wake up.

Leaving for school the next morning, Zeb saw his mother retrieving what was left of the vase. It had been a favorite of hers, an honorarium from the Women's Club for her service as chairperson of the hospital's auxiliary, but she hadn't cried

as she swept the pieces into a dustpan. Zeb stood at the end of the hall and watched without her sensing he was there, in that moment believing he would never again look at her with more than pity.

In school, he pled illness so the coach dismissed him from gym class. All week he concocted one excuse after another until the welts on his body were mere hints he camouflaged by snapping a towel at anyone who came close. That he never dated Amy again wasn't his choice. She was the one too busy to talk when he called, the one who turned away when he approached her in public. After a while he started seeing her with Nathan Wheeler, and when he asked around, he discovered she and Nathan were dating. Then he began watching Nathan, funneling the hatred he had been taught so effectively by his father. Waiting in the cemetery for Buck to deliver the goods, Zeb smiled when he heard the Pontiac come in off the street. Today was payback.

Chapter Four

Marta Amberson sat at her kitchen table staring out at her back yard for a long time after the school called. Rene had sounded a touch condescending, as if none of her children ever had any dealings with the law, which in truth they probably hadn't, but Marta knew the secretary's supercilious tone had more to do with husbands than anyone's children, foster or otherwise.

Long ago, early in their high school senior year, Rene and Marta met Ben Amberson at a party shortly after his family moved to town. Many girls were interested in the tall, lean stranger with lanky dark hair and brooding gypsy eyes, though it had been mainly Rene and Marta he spent time with at the party. When they ran into each other at the mall the next day, the girls had talked almost exclusively about Ben, Rene confiding plots she had devised to place herself in his proximity.

On Monday in school, the girls again ran into each other, this time in the restroom outside the library. Rene brought up the subject of Ben, her enthusiasm only slightly dampened. She had walked past his house and seen him tuning the engine of his car—a primer gray Ford Falcon, she reported somewhat disparagingly—and though she had dallied to talk, he hadn't stopped work while maintaining the barest veneer of politeness. Marta didn't mention that on Sunday afternoon Ben had come to her house and invited her to the school dance the following Friday, an invitation she had to refuse because her family was driving to Albuquerque to visit her grandparents. She had smiled at Ben and asked for a rain check he willingly gave, though they hadn't set any date.

The next Monday, after the weekend with her grandparents, Marta listened to Rene talk about how she had danced with Ben the previous Friday night, and how sexy he was and how she'd had almost as much fun as if it had been a date rather than just meeting up when they got there. Marta kept quiet, wondering if Ben would again ask her out.

The following Friday night they went to the movies and for Cokes before he took her home and said goodnight without once having compromised his gentleman's manners. After humming happily all weekend, on Monday Marta listened to Rene lament that Ben hadn't called her. Later that week, when they were alone in the restroom off the gym, Rene confided her heart, describing her loneliness and how unappealing she found most of the boys, making an exception of Ben and crediting the difference to his having grown up in Houston, a big city with a music and theater scene the likes of which Berrendo had never known. She pouted over Ben's apparent lack of interest whenever she accosted him in the halls, and almost cried when she said she guessed he had taken another girl out last weekend and wouldn't ever call her for a date.

Marta felt sorry for Rene, so again kept quiet, not wanting to hurt her more. It wasn't that they were close friends, just that Rene seemed to genuinely like Ben Amberson, and Marta could appreciate the disappointment she must feel that the interest wasn't mutual.

Later that day, Ben surprised Marta by coming up behind at her locker. She turned around and there he was, so close she could have kissed him without leaning far. They talked a while in the intimacy of their sheltered space amid the noise of Main Hall between classes. When the bell rang, he touched her cheek in parting and promised to call her that night. Feeling pleased beyond measure, she turned around and saw Rene watching with a shocked expression of betrayal. Marta had tried to smile, but Rene wasn't into reconciliation. Twenty years after the June they all graduated and Marta became Mrs. Amberson, Rene's voice still carried a grudge whenever the two women spoke.

It irritated Marta. From the beginning, even as far back as the first year they were married, when she had tried to tell Ben about it, he always responded, "That skinny girl with mousy hair?" His dismissal had made her feel badly for Rene all over again. But now, sitting in her kitchen trying to fathom why Nathan would be taken to the police station for questioning, Marta lost patience with Rene's petty vendetta, and with her patience went all semblance of sympathy for the secretary of Berrendo High.

Deciding not to wait the full hour, Marta walked to her bedroom to change out of her jeans and T-shirt. She tucked a white cotton blouse into her burgundy corduroy skirt while stepping sockless into a pair of loafers. In the bathroom she ran a brush through her curly brown hair and decided no more makeup than a touch of lipstick would be appropriate. Because the more respectable she looked, the more sway she could hope to have with the authorities, she returned to the bedroom and sat on a straight-backed chair to pull on a pair of pantyhose. Of course the authorities would know that her family had been instrumental in establishing the First Presbyterian Church in Berrendo a century ago, that her husband managed the largest insurance agency in the county, and that her own children displayed exemplary behavior in all aspects of life. Nathan was the son of people who had once been close friends of her and her husband's but were now almost strangers, though they were of pioneer stock, Marta knew that for a fact. Reassuring herself that Nathan was a good boy living with a good family, she reasoned it never hurt to put your best foot forward. One couldn't assume too much. She felt certain most mothers, whether foster or biological, experienced an uneasy fear any time they were called to a police station on their child's behalf. After all, the authorities, by definition, had the power to exact obedience, and Marta had always been a compliant citizen.

Her purse hanging from its strap on her shoulder and her car keys in her hand, she surveyed herself in the full-length mirror behind her bedroom door. Her small pie-shaped face with its short nose and thin lips smiled bravely at its own reflection, but her spirit was sinking at the thought of Nathan—who always tried so hard to be no trouble—alone in an interrogation room being bullied by a detective for a crime she knew in her heart the boy was too sweet to be capable of committing.

The Pontiac was close to Artesia by then, the penetrating stink from the refinery making Zeb nauseous behind the wheel. He looked into the rearview mirror to see a lopsided grin on Buck's stupid face.

"What're you smiling about?"

"Just feeling good 'cause everything's going so smooth," Buck answered in a placating tone.

"He still out?"

Buck looked at the kid on the floor. Nathan's face was flat on the dirty carpet, his glasses askew so a temple was off one ear. Because the kid hadn't moved since being hogtied, Buck was a little worried that he'd used too much ether but he didn't want to share his concern with his cousin if he could avoid it. His feet were resting on the kid's butt, humped over the drive shaft, and he could feel the kid breathing. To Zeb he said, "Like he was cold-cocked."

Zeb laughed. "That's what he's gonna be damn quick."

Buck grinned into the mirror, then looked at the huge refinery sprawling alongside the road. He had once hoped to get a job for one of the oil companies in Artesia, but knowing he would have to write down that he had served time discouraged him from applying. His affable grin was his only defense against rejection, and a smile could carry him just so far. About his only hope for a decent future lay with Zeb. Though doing his cousin's dirty work wasn't exactly what Buck had envisioned for his life, it would probably pay well and keep him close to home, which he saw as an advantage after a year in Denver had taught him the outside world was a vastly complicated place.

Zeb was thinking that after this he would have enough leverage to make Buck do anything. The way Zeb saw the world, power wasn't bestowed on those who followed the rules but on those who broke them without getting caught. One sure way to achieve that was to have a triggerman in your pocket, and he figured having one with a blood connection was as good as it got. If push came to shove, Buck could be manipulated by either a promise or a threat to change his parents' lives one way or another. Even if Buck didn't give a horse's ass for his parents, he wouldn't be able to implicate Zeb in any of what lay ahead without putting a noose around his own neck, and Zeb didn't think Buck was that stupid.

Glancing at the fuel gauge made Zeb reconsider. "What the fuck!" he shouted. "We're out of gas!"

"No way," Buck said, trying to slide over the fact that he hadn't thought to fill the tank.

"Look at the goddamn gauge!"

Leaning forward to peer over Zeb's shoulder, Buck put

more weight on his feet, squashing the kid so he moaned, which made Buck's neck prickle with sweat. "Guess we gotta make a pit stop," he mumbled, watching the kid on the floor.

Nathan lifted his head an inch or two, then let it fall, knocking his glasses all the way off. Buck picked them up and put them on, craning to see himself in the rearview mirror, but his reflection was too distorted through the lenses. "Hey, what d'ya think? Do I look like Buddy Holly?"

Zeb shot him a look of disgust unmistakable even through the distortion. "You're gonna have to get out and make sure no one comes near while I fill the tank."

"No problem." Buck took the glasses off, folded them shut and slid them into his shirt pocket. "The kid's starting to wake up, though."

Without breaking speed, Zeb leaned over the seat to look. "Kick him in the head."

Buck stared at him. "Don't you want him awake so he knows who's delivering the payback?"

"What I don't want is him yelling for help when we stop for gas."

Buck winced when he slammed the toe of his boot behind the kid's ear. Nathan let out a gust of air and slumped limp as Zeb pulled into an Exxon station. Before the car had completely stopped, Buck jumped out and slammed the door. Pacing back and forth halfway between the office and the pumps, he tried arguing that maybe they could say Nathan was sick, then realized if he was he'd be on the seat and Buck would be riding in front, not in back with his feet holding the kid down. The grease monkey in the garage could have noticed when they pulled in that Buck was in back with his knees to his chin. Anyone with sense would know that meant something bulky was under his feet.

The mechanic ambled out wiping his hands on a rag. He

glanced at Zeb at the pump but kept walking toward Buck. "Need something?"

Buck stopped pacing and shook his head.

The man turned toward Zeb.

"Stay away from that car!" Buck shouted.

The man looked over his shoulder at Buck, then backed toward the garage, still wiping his hands, his dark eyes sharp.

"It comes to ten dollars," Zeb yelled. "Pay him, Buck."

Buck looked at Zeb, wondering how his cousin could be so dumb as to use his name. But he pulled his wallet out and gave the man half of what was in it, then sprinted for the car, remembering only at the last minute to go around so when he got in the man wouldn't see the kid on the floor.

As Zeb burned rubber through the intersection, Buck looked back at the man holding the ten in one hand and the rag in the other, his mouth open and his eyes more than curious.

"Sonofabitch!" Buck said, turning around to meet Zeb's eyes in the rearview. "You told him my name!"

"No, I didn't," Zeb lied. "I said the gas came to ten bucks. You must've heard wrong."

Buck tried to remember, but couldn't say for sure. Beside him was the tie he'd worn as part of his charade. He picked it up and ran the wide end around the back of his neck, soaking up sweat. He threw the tie out, then swiveled around to watch it float on the wind before falling in the dust at the side of the road. When he turned back, Nathan stirred on the floor. Buck pressed his feet down on the kid's butt, took the glasses out of his pocket and put them on.

"The kid must be blind." He laughed with a new idea. "If we don't give his glasses back, he'll never know who we are."

"Throw 'em out the window."

Buck lifted the glasses to meet his cousin's eyes in the rearview. "I thought you wanted him to know who was hurting him."

Zeb smiled. "Paybacks can be anonymous."

Buck tossed the glasses out, then turned around and watched them bounce once before disappearing in the weeds. Too late he realized that left only him as an identifiable suspect. He reasoned that might be okay since he was experienced and could stand up to the kind of questioning cops dished out. Zeb was a softie, for all his mean ways, and sure to reward Buck for taking the heat.

Amy sat eating lunch with Nora while her eyes constantly scanned the crowded quad for any glimpse of Nathan. As she bit into the firm flesh of her pear, she remembered how he had offered his hand to help her climb off the bleachers. She had ignored the offer, jumping from five tiers up and landing so close she almost stepped on the toes of his spit-polished shoes. They had laughed, comfortable in their silence, but now, in the noise of almost the entire student body eating lunch in the quad—everyone, it seemed, except Nathan—she kept remembering his offer and wishing she could return to that moment and accept his help.

"Cheer up," Nora said, the curved lines of her platinum hair cupping her plum-lipsticked smile, "at least Zeb Mulroney's not here either."

Amy suddenly felt nauseous, remembering how Zeb had kicked Joe Mason so badly he was hospitalized. The scene had been terrifying, the knowledge that such brutality was dealt by the same boy she had spent the last two hours holding hands with in a dark theater. Thinking of it now made her glad her mother's lover was an ex-cop. The world was a more vicious place than most kids growing up in

Berrendo came close to suspecting, the town being normally so boring. Today was different. She felt a quiet foreboding, like the hum of locusts about to descend.

Setting her pear aside unfinished, she reapplied her ruby-red lipstick, then snapped her compact closed and stood up. "I think I'll go ask the nurse if Nathan went home sick."

"I'll go with you." Nora tossed her untouched lunch into the closest trash bin. Thin to the point of emaciation, she was on a perpetual diet to lose what she always called just five more pounds.

Lucinda sat alone at her kitchen table studying Devon's rental application. Instead of the scrawled handwriting of most men she knew, his was a stylized printing, bold with character. She saw that his former address was 1214 Stockwell Lane, El Paso, Texas, that he had resided there for ten years, and that he had left blank the space for previous address. His former employer was the El Paso Police Department, Crimes Against Persons Division, his supervisor Lieutenant Richard Dreyfus. Lucinda lifted the receiver of her cordless phone and punched in the area code for El Paso and then the number for the lieutenant's office.

After two rings, a man's voice answered, "Crimes Against Persons."

"Yes, hello," Lucinda waffled, not having rehearsed her approach. "I'm sorry to bother you." She mentally scolded herself for beginning with an apology. "My name is Lucinda Sterling and I have an apartment to rent here in Berrendo?" She chided herself for using a questioning tone when she hadn't yet presented a query. "I'm sorry. I don't seem to be making a very strong start here. Am I speaking with Lieutenant Dreyfus?"

"No, ma'am," the voice replied firmly. "The lieutenant's

on leave this week. I'm Sergeant Barger. Is there something I can help you with?"

"Yes, that is I hope so." She took a deep breath, then looked at the rental application while she spoke. "A Mr. Devon Gray has applied to rent my apartment, and he listed Lieutenant Dreyfus as a reference. I wonder if you knew Mr. Gray or could recommend him as a tenant?"

There was a momentary silence before Barger said, "Yeah, I knew him. I suppose he'd be a good tenant. Don't see why not. Wasn't any fiscal irresponsibility in his history that I know of."

She puzzled over his tone. "You don't sound entirely enthusiastic in your recommendation, Sergeant."

"I didn't like the man, but that's neither here nor there far as you're concerned."

"May I ask why you didn't like him?"

"He was a loner and police work's generally considered a team effort. Maybe that's all there was to it."

"I see. I suppose it's probably confidential, but can you tell me why he resigned?"

"Quit out of the blue. Left quite a few cases pending. Somebody else had to pick 'em up."

"I see," she said again, though she didn't. "Do you know the reason he gave for resigning?"

"Psychic fatigue is what he put on the paperwork, but to tell you the truth, Mrs. Sterling, if he hadn't resigned he would've been called before a court of inquiry to answer a few questions."

"About what?"

"His last case involved a prostitute charged with the death of her husband. Detective Gray was assigned as the investigating officer before we found out he'd been seeing the woman socially, if you know what I mean. He should've taken himself off the case from the git-go, but he stayed in there muddying the water till the officer assisting him was murdered. Gray resigned right after that, though he was the only one with enough knowledge to come close to arresting the perp. His resignation went down pretty hard around here. Most of us felt he should've stuck with it 'stead of leaving us with two unsolved homicides on the board."

"I see," she whispered.

"But as for your question, Mrs. Sterling, I don't see any reason why he wouldn't make a good tenant. He was a quiet man, not prone to partying, from what I know."

"Yes, thank you," she said weakly, then hung up.

The kitchen was silent, sunlight falling from the hall to shine on the terra cotta tile she herself had laid on the floor. The cabinets were white oak, the counter butcher block from one end to the other. Her warm, cozy kitchen where she felt most at home. If she stood up and looked out the window, she could see the converted garage she had rented to Devon on the misguided notion that she and Amy would actually be safer having him there.

Grabbing the rental application off the table, she stomped out of the house, letting the screen door bang behind her as she stalked across the yard. She wanted to barge in on him, but restrained herself to a knock she thought sounded only slightly melodramatic.

Fresh from a shower after their recent bout in bed, he opened the door with his dark shirt unbuttoned over a clean pair of jeans. His smile died as he stepped back to allow her in. She sailed across his threshold. Pivoting to face him, she threw the wadded application so it bounced off his chest and fell to the floor. He picked up the paper and flattened its wrinkles, scanning it longer than it must have taken him to recognize what it was, then met her eyes.

"I called your reference," she spit out, so angry she wanted to attack him with her fists.

"Dreyfus?"

"He was on leave. I spoke with a Sergeant Barger."

Comprehension dawned in his eyes. "I don't suppose he had anything good to say."

She hesitated, belatedly remembering Barger had begun by saying he'd never liked Devon. But she doubted the sergeant would lie. "He said you use prostitutes! That you were involved with one who committed a murder you were investigating."

Devon dropped the crumpled application on the table, then turned his back and stared out at the yard as he buttoned his shirt and tucked in its tails. When he faced her again, his expression was pained. "I'm sorry you didn't talk to Dreyfus."

"What would he have told me?"

"Nothing about my sex life, I'm sure of that."

"I don't care about the sergeant's lack of discretion, Devon. We didn't even use a condom!"

Relief flashed on his face. "Is that what you're worried about?"

"Don't you think it's worthy of worry?"

He laughed. "Yeah, don't get me wrong. I'm not making light of your feelings, it's just that I was taking this in a whole different direction."

"What other direction is there? Do you already have AIDS and don't care who you infect?"

"I don't have AIDS."

"How do you know? Have you been tested? Even if you have, was it more than once? It can show up a lot later, you know. It takes more than one test."

"I've been tested twice, but the only thing happening between me and that prostitute was oral sex, and I always used protection."

"Oh that's a lovely picture."

He sighed. "It's a long story, Lucinda. I guess I knew I'd have to tell you someday, but I didn't think it'd be like this."

"Maybe I don't want to hear it. God, I can't believe how much I trusted you!" He looked so hurt she wanted to relent but couldn't. "When I think of you spending time with Amy, it makes me cringe. Can you understand that?"

"It was one prostitute, not anything I make a habit of."

She took a step backward and sat down on the coffee table, covering her face with her hands as she tried not to cry.

He kept his distance. She gave him credit for that. When she had pulled herself together enough to look up, he was standing in the open door, watching her.

"It was bad luck," he said, "your getting Barger instead of Dreyfus."

She sniffed. "I thought cops always stick together."

"I'm not one of them anymore."

She nodded. "He said something about a cop getting killed and how you let the department down by resigning right afterwards."

"I'll tell you anything you want to know about the prostitute, but I'm not ready to talk about the rest of it."

She looked away, seeing a library book on the table beside her, a novel called *The Joke*. "You like Kundera?"

"I haven't started it yet. Do you think I'll like it?"

"I did." She met his eyes again. "Can't you pick up women in bars whenever you want?"

"Probably."

"So why see a prostitute?"

"All I wanted was oral sex."

"You've never asked me to do it."

" 'Cause I don't like it." He glanced around, then met her eyes. "Two women I'd been close to thought there was something wrong with me 'cause I wouldn't let 'em do that. So I did it with a hooker, trying to figure out why I didn't like it."

"What did you find out?"

"Watching a woman do that puts her in a position of subservience, and that's not what I want."

She smiled, feeling better about him again. "Would you like to come into the house for coffee?"

"I could use some."

When Marta Amberson walked into the lobby of the police station, the uniformed woman behind the glass partition wearily watched her approach.

"Excuse me," Marta said into the round opening above a scooped-out tray for the passage of documents. "I was told to ask for Detective Fuller."

The woman frowned. "We don't have any officer named Fuller, detective or otherwise."

Confused, all Marta could think to do was repeat herself. "I was told to ask for Detective Fuller."

"By who?"

"Rene Donnor, the secretary at Berrendo High. She called and said Detective Fuller was taking my foster son out of school and bringing him here for questioning, that I should pick him up in an hour. It hasn't been an hour, but if Nathan's in trouble . . ." She stopped, realizing she had answered more than was asked.

"Have a seat," the woman said, reaching for a phone. "Someone will be out to help you."

The woman looked worried, which disconcerted Marta.

Her request seemed easily understandable, yet from the expression on the woman's face, something was drastically wrong.

"This looks right," Buck said.

Zeb couldn't believe how stupid his cousin was. Buck had suggested this place, then couldn't find it. Just because the tavern was closed, its blown-down sign shattered into splinters and its eroded driveway choked with weeds, the building hadn't moved. Yet Zeb had driven past the setback cinder block twice before Buck decided it must be the place. Zeb parked in back and looked at the door to his future.

It was cracked, weathered a dull gray, slightly ajar. When he pushed it with his forefinger, the door creaked open, revealing a dusty concrete floor, a hall leading to darkness, and an open walk-in cooler long abandoned to the desert heat. Zeb thought a dungeon couldn't have been better. The dereliction of the place fit with his anticipation of what it should look like: the pit of a private combustion that would burn his rage to ashes. Maybe on his way out he'd dab dust on his forehead like Catholics did at Lent, signifying the purification of his soul. Turning back to his cousin standing on the far side of the car, he said, "Bring him in."

Buck opened the back door and dragged the unconscious body out, then gently hefted it onto his shoulder. Zeb marveled at Buck's strength, something he himself hadn't developed much, probably because he ditched gym class so often. But in his mind, muscle could be hired, so why break a sweat? "Dump him on the floor in the cooler," he said.

Scanning the barren horizon and what he could see of the road, empty for miles in both directions, he tried to smile but his lip lifted in a snarl instead. He followed his cousin inside the dim, dusty ruin where they both stood staring down at the kid just beginning to stir. "Get the stuff," Zeb muttered.

Buck went back out to the car, so Zeb was alone when Nathan opened his eyes. Their fear turned Zeb on. He kicked Nathan in the gut, heard his yelp and watched spit drool from his mouth to change the dust to mud. Zeb hunkered on his heels and dabbed a finger in it, touched Nathan's cheek, and drew a closed circle. When this was over, he'd be clean again, his anger dispelled in one final conflagration so hot no residue could remain.

Buck came back and dumped their tools from the bag to the floor. "What one you want first?"

Zeb glanced around, his eyes having adjusted enough that he could see into the far corner where a wreath of wire hung on the wall. He had to force his mouth closed enough to say, "Pliers."

Chapter Five

Alicia Mulroney stood in the open door and surveyed her son's bedroom with less than joy. The carpeting was the same pale champagne as in the hall, but the walls here were mocha, the furniture of English oak so old it was almost black. With the taupe drapes closed along the wall facing the door, the room looked like a sepia print from long ago. Yet it was the room of a teenage boy.

Nervously, Alicia looked over her shoulder to glance up and down the hall. She was alone in the house, even the maid had gone for groceries, but the men her life revolved around were unpredictable, often returning without warning. She reasoned that a mother had a right to be in her son's bedroom, even to search it. Her argument, however, did nothing to allay her fear as she crossed the threshold and closed the door.

She began with the bed, lifting each pillow, sliding her hand between the mattress and box springs, getting down on her knees to look underneath. The drawer in the bedside table revealed a pack of Camel cigarettes, a tiny gold lighter inside a small clear ashtray, a baggie of marijuana, and the kind of rolling papers that held a wire inside each sheet to serve as a built-in roach clip. Pushed behind those things was a white leather address book. She sat on the edge of the bed and opened the book to discover it was blank. Not one single name or number written anywhere. Leafing through the empty pages made her wonder what could be wrong with her son that he had no friends, then realized it reflected the hermitage of her own life. Despite being active in what passed for society in Berrendo, she had no confidante, neither here nor back in Texas. The bitterness of her marriage had left her marooned, and she supposed she might have kept Zeb there, too. She replaced his book in the drawer, slid it closed and looked around.

The closet was no doubt a haven of vast possibilities, but it was immense, covering one entire wall, and she found the prospect of searching it formidable. She moved instead to the black leather recliner and opened the octagonal table beside it. Inside she found a collection of videos. That they were pornography didn't dismay her, though the illustrations of spankings were a little unsettling. Given his upbringing, however, she was surprised he didn't dissect dogs or burn cats as his recreational pastime.

Buried in the back of the table's interior, she found an eight-by-five photo album plump with pictures. She sat on the ottoman and opened the book, immediately recognizing that the first photo was of Amy Sterling talking with a girl who flaunted platinum hair and heroin makeup. Alicia turned the page to see more pictures of Amy, all taken from a distance while she was apparently unaware of being photographed. Alicia kept turning the pages, amazed to see only Amy. Some of the pictures had been taken through her bedroom window, evidently by means of a telephoto lens.

"The little devil," she chuckled, amused her son had formed such an attachment to a girl he had dated only briefly. She wondered how often he looked at the photos, and then if his keeping them with his pornography meant he used them for the same purpose. That put a more vicious twist on his attachment, maybe even pushing it into obsession. Disturbed by that thought, Alicia returned the album and closed the table, then looked around again.

If he kept his drugs at his bedside and his porno by his TV chair, what did he keep with his underclothes? Steeling herself, she crossed the room and opened the drawer. The condoms were no surprise, though their quantity was. She snorted with disdain, thinking he would have to fuck every girl in town twice to exhaust that supply. She closed the drawer filled with dozens of pairs of jockey shorts, then opened his sock drawer. A thorough search revealed nothing other than socks. Undaunted she moved through drawer after drawer of sweaters and sweats, coming up empty-handed. She looked at the desk but knew from experience that it was locked.

With a sigh, she opened one end of his closet and started searching each garment, eventually finding what she wanted in the breast pocket of the brown Armani jacket his grandmother had given him for Christmas the year before. Holding the key hidden in the palm of her hand, she opened the door and stepped into the hall, then stood a long time listening for any sound that might indicate she was no longer alone.

The four bedrooms and baths on the second story and the nine rooms on the ground floor all quivered with silence, as if the house itself were conspiring with her. This time she left the door open when she entered her son's domain. A mother, after all, could justify being in his closets and drawers, but his desk was another matter entirely. Especially a son with such means, she thought with a smile as she used her red lacquered nails to smoothly slide his bankbook from its niche.

Quickly she opened it to the last entry. Despite a hefty withdrawal made only yesterday, the balance was still over ten thousand dollars. She felt certain Albert Lacrosse at the bank would grant her request without asking questions. She was a co-signer on Zeb's account, although technically both signatures were required for any withdrawal over a thousand.

Noting Zeb had taken out exactly that amount yesterday, she wondered what he had done with the money. It seemed too much to spend on drugs in the local market.

Suddenly she laughed, suspecting he had used the money to get a girl out of trouble. She wondered if such things happened anymore, what with Planned Parenthood dispensing abortions on demand. If that had been the case when Zeb was conceived, she certainly wouldn't have married his father. She'd had her pick of suitors, all as wealthy as Silas Mulroney and most better looking. There had even been one she wanted, at least she had thought so. Grant dos Passos was his name, and she had imagined herself his wife more than once. But despite moving in the same circles and frequently seeing each other at parties, Grant never asked her out. The scion of a prestigious family in Paraguay, he was rumored to be engaged to a girl chosen by his father. Occasionally, savoring the scraps of her memories, Alicia wondered if Grant's marriage had turned out as empty as hers.

Her hasty wedding had been the result of what today would be called date rape but back then was considered a young man getting out of hand. When she found herself caught after being nailed, she followed the rules laid down by his religion, though she couldn't help wonder where his sanctity had been when he was indulging in sex before marriage. She understood fornication to be as much a sin in the Church as abortion, maybe not as serious but equally a sin. That notwithstanding, Catholic boys were apparently expected to harvest any wild seeds sown in the furrows of virtue, and the fact that Silas was subsequently disowned for marrying a girl his father disapproved of was God's little joke.

It had taken nearly twenty years of brown-nosing to get her husband halfway reinstated into his father's good graces, and that only in the form of gifts, not entitlements. Her house was one. A mansion by most standards, it was a crumb of charity among the oil-rich Mulroneys. So here she stood, the former Miss Alicia Hollander, whose own fortune had been sacrificed to saving her pride by propping up her husband's failing law firm, now about to steal money from her son. She would flee to La Jolla and sue for divorce under the skies of California, which shone with much more warmth on financially devastated women.

Carrying her son's bankbook, she descended the stairs, taking a last look at the house she had resented since moving in, then walked out to the garage where her Mercedes waited with her suitcases already locked in the trunk. Without a backward glance, she left marriage and motherhood behind.

The Settlers Bank of Berrendo was in a pueblo revival building, squat and flat-roofed with a corbel above the elaborately carved wood front door. Luminous in her natural silk jacket over an ivory shell and snug charcoal skirt, Alicia glided across the faux rustic lobby and directly into the office of the president, whose door had been momentarily left open.

Albert Lacrosse wiped the irritation off his face, rose and extended his hand, ready to shake with her or gesture toward the visitor's chair, whichever seemed more likely to be accepted. She took the chair and smoothed her short skirt over her lean thighs, crossing her legs so the hem rode up well past her knees. Pleased to see him admiring her figure, she gave herself a brief moment to study his face, the heavy dark brows dwarfing his beetle eyes, the broad flattened nose, the thick lips she had allowed to kiss her last year at the United Way Christmas Ball. Silas had been insufferable that night, arriving already drunk, and Albert, with his banker's sensitivity, had escorted her out to the terrace and down its stairs to amble along the banks of the country club's artificial lake, both of them taking in the refreshing night air with relief. It had been there that Alicia allowed him to kiss her. Opposing him across his desk in the early afternoon of what she hoped would be her last day in town, she let the memory of that kiss drip from her lips as she smiled at the man who in all other circumstances she considered odious.

He leaned back in his chair with the smile of an underling who thought himself superior as she removed her son's passbook from her purse and said, "I've decided to transfer Li'l Zeb's money into the joint savings belonging to Silas and me."

"You mean the joint account that's nearly empty?" he asked, as if her name was on more than one.

"I don't remember the balance," she lied.

He shuttered his thoughts behind a facile smile.

She flourished the passbook. "It's far too much for a boy his age. I think it best that his father and I monitor his expenditures."

"I'm sorry, Alicia," Albert said with feigned regret. "You're no longer a signatory on that account."

She waited, pertly poised with a coy smile belying her panic.

"Li'l Zeb transferred guardianship to his grandfather several months ago." He smiled. "The bank sent you a letter. Probably you set it aside without reading it."

"How could the transfer be effected without my signature?"

"Perhaps you signed the document without realizing what it was."

She struggled to hide her anger.

"If you need money," he said in a conciliatory tone, "I could arrange an unsecured loan for up to ten thousand with only a few phone calls."

"Whom would you call?"

"Your father-in-law's accountant approves all unsecured loans, and your husband would have to be informed. Is that a problem?"

Tossing the bankbook on his desk, she rose with as much dignity as she could summon. "Since that's useless to me, I leave it in your trust."

"Please don't." He, too, rose, picked up the passbook and extended it toward her. "Li'l Zeb will no doubt be wanting it."

"Did it ever occur to you, Albert, that a woman might need money independent of the men in her life?"

"Absolutely. But in such a case, she should have her own and not ask for theirs."

"You son of a bitch," she whispered.

He smiled. "I believe that's the definition of my job, Mrs. Mulroney."

Clutching the passbook, she walked out, commanding herself to cross the lobby with enough composure that the tarts behind the tellers' windows couldn't guess she had been denied.

Inside her car, she forced herself not to cry, not wishing to spoil her makeup. After several minutes of watching the flag flap above the post office across the street, she decided the pity on her son's face the last time they had shared an honest moment might induce him to finance her flight from the family.

Walking into the school's office with studied aplomb, Alicia smiled at Rene Donnor talking on the phone at her secretary's desk. Being the widow of a man who hadn't left adequate insurance, Rene was forced to work, and Alicia had always felt sorry for her. For herself, she felt keenly that widowhood would be a desirable status, especially since Silas's many faults didn't include a lack of life insurance.

Not wanting to appear frantic enough to hurry Rene off the phone, Alicia glanced at the bulletin board full of college scholarship announcements and applications for financial aid. Rene was soon finished and asking if there was something Alicia wanted. She turned around and smiled. "I was hoping to see my son," she paused to scrunch her nose in a gesture of frivolity, "for just a tiny minute."

Rene stared too long, making Alicia suspect the secretary knew her need was far from frivolous. In an understated tone, Rene finally asked, "Wasn't it you who called this morning to say he was ill?"

Dumfounded, Alicia shook her head.

"I so seldom speak with you on the phone," Rene said, "I had no reason to suspect whoever did was an imposter."

Alicia tried to collect herself, guessing that Zeb was playing hooky and suspecting, if she made an issue of it, her pose of frivolity would be unmasked. "It must have been his grandmother," she said, then laughed, congratulating herself on her quick wits. "We're both Mrs. Mulroney, after all."

"Yes, you are," Rene agreed, though her eyes still flickered with doubt.

"Zeb did stay with his grandparents last night, but I had no idea they'd kept him out of school today."

Rene's smile was noncommittal.

"I'll drive over there and find out why." She wanted to say something to defuse Rene's suspicions that things weren't quite right, but just then someone opened the door and she turned around, following Rene's gaze.

Amy Sterling stood on the threshold in a red silk blouse much too risqué for a girl her age. Remembering the photos in her son's room, Alicia assessed the girl's figure in the tight blouse, poured-on jeans, and platform sneakers that made her legs look longer than they already were. If allowances were made for the bruised style of makeup currently in fashion, Alicia was forced to concede her son had good taste in feminine beauty. "Hello, Amy," she said with a smile. "I haven't seen you in ages."

"No, ma'am," Amy answered politely, then shifted her gaze to the secretary. "Do you know if Nathan Wheeler went home sick, Mrs. Donnor?"

Rene seemed at a loss for words, making Alicia think something very strange was happening. Before any more could be said, Marta Amberson walked in with two men. Alicia recognized them as the police detectives who had investigated a burglary at her home a few months back. They, in turn, recognized her, glanced at Amy, then focused on Rene. Alicia looked at her, too, noting her complexion had paled considerably. The door to the vice principal's office opened and Tom Barrow emerged carrying a sheaf of papers. Though he had been about to speak, he closed his mouth without uttering a sound. Alicia took a step back, instinctively regretting that her mere presence had inserted Zeb into whatever ugly situation was about to unfold.

Hannah McGraw, the receptionist in the law office of Mulroney and Broussard, smiled as Mrs. Mulroney walked in, but her smile quickly faded in response to the odd expression on the woman's face. Mrs. Mulroney was almost laughing, barely able to restrain herself, and the edge of hysterics under the surface of her taut control made the receptionist wary. She picked up the phone and buzzed Mr. Mulroney's secretary before Alicia spoke.

"Tell Mr. Mulroney his wife's here," Hannah said, smiling at the woman in front of her.

"He's on the phone," Jane Dorrie answered curtly, knowing Hannah could see that his line was in use.

Hannah leaned down as if fixing her shoe and whispered, "I don't think she's well."

There was a silence, then Jane said, "I'll be right out."

Hannah hung up and smiled at the boss's wife.

Alicia was biting her lip now, her eyes blazing with some thought she evidently found hilarious.

Jane opened the door and said, "Please come in, Mrs. Mulroney."

Alicia studied her husband's secretary, a red-haired, green-eyed beauty no doubt chosen for her looks. Laughing a goodbye to Hannah, she preceded Jane across the office shared by the two secretaries, noting that Geoff Broussard had chosen a blonde in pink lipstick to accompany him through his days. She flung open the door to her husband's office so it banged against the wall, and both secretaries looked at each other as they heard her derisive laugh just before she slammed the door.

Alicia flounced into the chair in front of his desk and laughed again.

"I cut short an important telephone conference," Silas said. A dark, swarthy man who carried too much weight, he wasn't amused. "Do you mind explaining why you're here?"

"Oh, in a minute. I've been laughing so hard I have to catch my breath." She continued to giggle as she watched him squirm.

"Perhaps you'd like a drink to quiet your nerves."

"It'll be yours that need quieting," she predicted.

"Albert called. Are you leaving town? Is that why you wanted money?"

She shook her head. "I was, but I've decided to stay and watch the mighty Mulroneys beg for mercy."

"What're you talking about?"

She laughed again, then said with undisguised glee, "Nathan Wheeler's been kidnapped."

"Who's he?"

"Amy Sterling's boyfriend."

"And who is Amy Sterling?"

"The girl Li'l Zeb's obsessed with. I was in his room earlier and found an entire album stuffed with photos he's taken without her knowing. What a devious little monster you've created, Silas."

"I think I should call your doctor. You seem in need of sedation."

She hooted her amusement so shrilly he looked at the door.

"Alicia, please. Have some sense of decorum."

"I wonder how much Zeb's showing poor Nathan right now. And Buck's helping him. We all know how much decorum Cousin Buck has."

"Will you tell me what in the hell you're talking about?"

She sat on the edge of her chair and leaned closer. "They've kidnapped Nathan Wheeler from school."

"What for?"

She leaned back, pleased with his angry bewilderment. "Your guess is as good as mine. I was in the office when Marta Amberson came in with two detectives. First Amy came in and asked for Nathan, then Marta showed up with the police, and poor Rene turned quite pale. It seems a man matching Buck's description walked in and asked for the boy, and Rene and Tom Barrow just handed him over. I got out before they could connect the fact that Li'l Zeb's playing hooky. But they'll make the connection, Silas, you can bank on that." She giggled at her choice of words.

Chapter Six

Marta Amberson sat on the bench along the wall in the school office watching the others flounder in what could best be called confusion. Rene Donnor and Tom Barrow were skewered on guilt, while the policemen had allowed themselves to be blinded by anger. Detective Saavedra, the slim-hipped dark one, had his badge in his hand, as if he thought showing it to Tom over and over would change the fact that the vice principal had failed to check the imposter's I.D. Marta kept wishing they wouldn't waste time on accusations. Wherever Nathan was, he needed help, and these buffoons seemed as incompetent as comedians dropped into the crucible of a tragedy.

Amy, sitting beside her, whispered, "Do you think I could call my mother?"

"I think you should," Marta whispered back. "Ask permission first."

Amy nodded and stood up. "Excuse me." She waited until everyone was watching her. "May I call my mother, please?"

"Certainly, Amy," Rene cooed, making Marta think she was more a dispenser of ointments than the preventer of wounds.

"Use my phone," Tom offered, gesturing toward his office.

Marta watched the girl go in and close the door. She liked Lucinda Sterling and would welcome her company in what lay ahead. Soon she would have to call Ben and, eventually, Hobb and Glenda Wheeler, though she hoped she could postpone telling Nathan's parents until he was home safe. She couldn't imagine what they would say, but poor Ben would be as worried as she was, and she hoped to delay telling him until the majority of his workday was over. Revenues from his agency weren't meeting corporate expectations, so this wasn't coming at a good time. Not that there was ever a good time for trouble, but he had recently developed an ulcer, and she made a point of trying not to add to his anxiety.

This knowledge, however, was a tremendous burden to carry alone. When her children learned what had happened to Nathan, they would be frightened, for themselves as well as him. All the children in town would be scared, the parents horrified that such a thing could happen. Appalled at the concentric circles of harm she could see rippling from the hurt sinking her heart, Marta walked to the counter that separated her from the two school officials she considered responsible for what had happened.

"Can you tell me," she asked bluntly of Tom Barrow, "the district's policy on releasing children to strangers?"

Tom looked stricken, but she forged ahead. "It can't be right," she accused, "to allow just anyone to come in off the street and take a child out of school!"

"No, it isn't," he said. "Believe me, Marta, I feel as badly about this as you do."

"I doubt that. I'm sure you're worried about your job, Tom, but I love Nathan. How could you let that poor boy be taken without even asking for identification?"

"I had every reason," Tom replied meekly, "to believe the man would have shown me a badge if I'd asked."

"You had every reason to ask!"

The detectives were watching, their faces pained with sympathy, while Rene stared as if she were gloating. Marta tried to tell herself she was being unfair, but the word only served to break the dam of her control. Turning back to Tom, she demanded, "Tell me the district's policy!"

It was Rene who said, "The pertinent policy requires that we get permission from a parent or guardian before allowing a police officer to take a student off campus. I called you myself, Marta."

"You didn't ask permission, you told me he was gone!"

Marta blinked back tears as she fumbled in her purse for a tissue. She blew her nose, the noise loud in the silence, then looked at Rene. "I never would've thought this of you. All these years you've carried a grudge, and I thought you petty because of it, but I never suspected you'd stoop so low as to gloat now when it's Nathan you've hurt more than me, though I feel like you've broken my heart." She looked at Tom. "Both of you!"

The door to Tom's office opened and Amy stood there looking distraught. For the girl's sake, Marta pulled herself together. She walked over to the bench and sat down to blow her nose again. Amy sat beside her and hugged her close, as if the woman were a child and the child was grown.

"They're coming," Amy whispered.

Marta put her tissue away and snapped her purse closed before asking, "Who?"

"My mother and Devon Gray. He's been renting our garage apartment all summer, and I asked her to bring him 'cause he's a retired cop from El Paso."

"What kind of cop?"

Amy swallowed before whispering against the catch in her throat, "A homicide detective."

Lucinda faced Devon at the kitchen table and said with soft entreaty, "Amy wants us both at school."

"Why?"

"Something about Nathan being in trouble." She went into the dining room and came back with her purse, then looked up from fishing her keys out. "I have a bad feeling about this, Devon. If you'd rather not get involved, I'll do my best to help Amy understand." Having carried their coffee cups to the sink, he watched her from there in silence, which compelled her to add, "Whatever's wrong has something to do with the police."

"Which might mean I'll be able to help," he said.

She smiled her gratitude, walking through the door he held open.

When she had backed her car out of the driveway and stopped in the street to change gears, he asked, "Why don't you tell me about Nathan?"

"I grew up with his parents," she said, driving slowly. "They got married right out of high school, but that wasn't unusual. Not many of the kids in my class went to college." She glanced at Devon, watching her so intensely she felt herself blush.

He smiled. "What're you thinking right now?"

"That I'm hedging. Most of the kids did get married right out of high school, but I wasn't one of them. Amy's what some people call a love child."

His smile became more sympathetic. "I'm surprised you didn't move to a big city where you could be anonymous."

"I'd already done that by going to the state college in Cruces and then library school in Tucson. It was a few years after I got back that I started dating Amy's father. He was killed in a car wreck before I knew I was pregnant." She braked for the stop sign on 8th, peering past the row of cypress that nearly blocked her view. "I think most people assumed Lyle would have married me if he'd lived, plus he was well-liked, and they were glad to think at least his child would still be around. I took advantage of all that good will and rode out the storm."

"Was there a storm?"

She nodded, easing through the intersection. "My parents were Baptists. And they were old." She half-laughed. "I came along as a late surprise and they, well, they were too set in their ways to accommodate a child. I'm not saying they were bad parents."

"Judging by you, they were pretty good ones."

She smiled. "They both died before Amy started school. After they were gone, Lyle's parents adopted me so we'd all have the same name."

"They sound like nice people."

She nodded. "They moved to Arizona a few years ago. That's their house we're living in." She laughed, embarrassed. "Now that I've unburdened myself, where were we?"

"Nathan's parents."

She stopped at the red light on 2nd. "His father was Hobb Wheeler, the descendent of a local pioneer family hereabouts. They had some money and sent Hobb to UNM. Glenda wanted to go, too, but she was already pregnant. She went to Albuquerque with him, of course, but just sat around the apartment and stewed most of the time. Not too long after Nathan was born, she developed a severe case of arthritis. Hobb started out to be a pharmacist, but when she got sick, he had to forget about graduate school. They came back here and he was hired as a traveling salesman by a pharmaceutical company. After that, he just sort of drifted away. His parents sold their ranch and moved to Connecticut to be close to Hobb's sister. I guess that pulled him toward the east coast."

The light changed. She crossed 2nd and drove down a block that was half commercial and half old homes now divided into apartments, then turned left on 1st, a street lined with small businesses. "Hobb met someone else and divorced Glenda when Nathan was about seven or eight. I don't think Nathan has a whole lot of contact with him. Glenda's father died about ten years ago, and her mother died, let's see, I guess it was last March. When Glenda moved back to Albuquerque to live in a home that caters to people like her, Nathan stayed here to finish high school. He lives with Marta and Ben Amberson. They're not officially his foster parents, but that's what everyone calls them. In reality they were simply good friends with Hobb and Glenda a long time ago."

She pulled into the lot behind the police station and parked near the door, then shut off the engine and faced him with a wry smile. "I didn't tell you much about Nathan. He's a nice kid, quiet and a good student. Joined ROTC because he's hoping the Army will pay his way through college. He's an Eagle Scout, and he attends the Presbyterian Church, but that's probably because Marta and Ben go there. I don't remember Glenda or Hobb being particularly religious, though they were married in the Methodist Church. I went to their wedding."

She stopped, noting he was no longer watching her but studying the façade of the police station. A giant masonry arch capped the glass doors, giving the two-story building a flighty appearance. In explanation, she said, "It used to be a bank. The city bought it about five years ago."

He looked at her again. "How long has Amy been dating Nathan?"

"Just this last summer. She was going with Zeb Mulroney before that, but I like Nathan better."

"Why?"

She looked across the street at the eight-story Petroleum Building, the closest to a high-rise the city could claim. "Zeb's family owns that and half of the rest of Berrendo. He's been spoiled in the worst way." She thought a moment. "Maybe because Nathan was essentially abandoned by his parents, he values people, takes life seriously." She shrugged, meeting Devon's eyes. "I like him a lot."

"You ready to go in?"

With a sudden chill, she whispered, "This is the police station. Amy's at school." She started her engine and backed out of the space, then glanced at him as she shifted into drive. "That was a creepy mistake."

"Jumping the gun," he agreed.

Pete Reck also found himself where he hadn't intended to go. Without remembering the path he had walked, he suddenly looked across the street and saw Lucinda Sterling's yellow stucco house under its towering old elms. Quickly glancing around, he saw no one on the neighboring porches, so allowed himself to wander as if aimlessly across the street. He stopped on the sidewalk and looked around again. Keenly aware that someone unseen could be watching, he walked up to the front door as if he had business with the lady who lived there. He rang the bell and peered in through the three narrow windows above the mail slot. Inside was a bare oak floor, an old camel-backed sofa covered with a rose-striped print and a round claw-foot piano stool serving as an end table. On top of it was a blue glass ashtray, and above the sofa hung a painting of a girl whose face was illuminated by the candle she held with both hands to shelter its flame from wind. To the left of the door he could just make out the corner of a bookcase, though he couldn't read any titles.

He wished he could be welcomed into this house, that he could sit on that sofa and read the books while sipping coffee or cocoa, maybe with a fire in the hearth at the north end of the room, which he knew was there because of the chimney on the outside wall. A woman like Lucinda would be cooking in the kitchen, and later, when it was dark outside and he'd made his rounds of locking the doors and checking the windows, he and the woman would go into the bedroom and do what married people did.

He glanced at the window to the right of the front door. It was shuttered inside with impenetrable mini-blinds. Beyond the blinds were probably draperies, and even if he could see past them, he suspected a woman like Lucinda might have curtains on her bed so her privacy under the covers would be guaranteed. Not that he expected her to be prudish, but she had a delicacy that suggested an uncommon degree of modesty.

He walked around to the south side of the house where a rock wall was closed by an arched wooden gate, too high for him to see into the yard. The neighbor's house was hidden behind pyrancantha bushes as thick as a hedge. He wondered who lived there, and if they knew how lucky they were to be able to watch Lucinda come and go without anyone taking note they were watching. Feeling certain someone had taken note of him, he ambled back to the sidewalk and continued the way he'd been going.

That the neighborhood was old was evidenced by the huge trees. The houses, too, were from another era. A few had pillars on their porches, some were built of brick, some of native limestone. As he progressed toward 2nd Street, the houses became older and larger. Just before he reached the busy intersection, he walked through a block of converted apartments and small businesses. Then he was on 2nd and commercial trucks lumbered by. He didn't wait for the light but caught enough of a break to dart across. Now he was in a neighborhood that was just as old but had always been more modest. The houses here were restored adobes and frame cottages squatting around a few Victorian queens looming over their minions.

Continuing south until he reached the Hondo River, he jumped from the bridge into the dry, narrow channel, then walked west along the sandy riverbed. In a curve of the bank was a niche he had found several days earlier. He settled his pack into the hollow and sat down leaning against it with his legs stretched out in front of him. If the river was running, he could serve as a dam until the current washed him into the Pecos and from there all the way to the Gulf of Mexico and eventually the Atlantic Ocean where he'd end up in the belly of a beast.

Because she had mistakenly gone to the police station first, Lucinda walked into the high school with a strong sense of dread. Seeing her daughter's pale face increased her foreboding.

Amy jumped up and ran to hug her mother. "Oh, Mom," she whispered, "Nathan's been kidnapped!"

Lucinda looked over Amy's head at Marta Amberson, watching them from where she sat on the wooden bench against the wall. Marta had been crying, giving credence to Amy's unbelievable statement. Lucinda looked at Rene Donnor, Tom Barrow and three men she didn't know, all watching from the other side of the counter. Holding onto Amy's hand, she introduced herself. When their eyes shifted to the man who had come in behind her, she said, "This is Devon Gray, a friend of mine."

Two of the men came forward and introduced themselves as Alex Saavedra and Dalton Wylie, detectives with the Berrendo Police Department.

In reply, Devon said, "I'm a retired detective from the El Paso P.D."

Saavedra, the dark one evidently in charge, asked, "Which division?"

"Homicide," Devon said softly.

Rene Donnor declared shrilly, "No one's said anything about that!" She looked helplessly at Tom Barrow. "It's not about that, is it, Tom?"

"Why, no," he answered in a tone of surprise, looking at Devon as if accusing him of upsetting everyone.

"I'm here simply as Mrs. Sterling's friend," he said.

"No sense putting the cart before the horse," Wylie told the room at large.

Lucinda sat down beside Marta. They shared the commiseration of mothers in such situations, though Lucinda felt fortunate to have her daughter within reach. When she again looked at Amy, however, she couldn't help notice that the red silk blouse had been finished in a style she hadn't anticipated.

Oblivious to her mother's observation, Amy was watching Devon watch the detectives, who in turn seemed to be watching him, as if everyone in the room were batting glances around like hot tamales.

Finally Saavedra indicated the gray-haired man sitting behind an easel. "This is Alan Auden, a police artist. We're trying to come up with a likeness of the suspect so we can get a clue of where to start looking."

Amy watched Devon lean against the wall near the door. She stood up and walked over to stand in front of him. "Thank you for coming."

He nodded, his gaze lingering on the deep cleavage revealed by the low cut of her blouse.

"This doesn't make sense," she whispered. "Why would anyone kidnap Nathan?"

"We'll get to the bottom of it. Go sit with your mother."

She turned away, obeying for the first time what she had

missed in not having a father: the command of a caring man asserting control.

Nestled between her mother and Mrs. Amberson, Amy wondered if all the crucial men in her life were destined to die young, then scolded herself for giving up on Nathan. As the detective had said, there was no sense in jumping to conclusions, no matter how discouraged she felt.

Mrs. Donnor told the artist, "His top lip was thinner, and his jawline was stronger."

"That's right," Mr. Barrow said.

"More eyebrows," Mrs. Donnor murmured.

"And he had the beginning of jowls," Mr. Barrow added.

Saavedra objected. "I thought you said he was in his mid-twenties."

"But he was fat."

"Stocky," Mrs. Donnor agreed.

The scratching of the artist's pencil was the only sound until suddenly a bell rang in the hall, making everyone jump. It was followed by the slamming of doors and a clamor of voices. Amy listened to her classmates going about their lives in ignorance of what had happened. Even Nora, who had accompanied her to the nurse's office but gone on to class when Amy came here. Nora would be looking for her at their lockers, maybe thinking this day was turning out to be strange since everyone kept disappearing.

Mr. Barrow walked out and closed the door, though Amy could see his silhouette against the frosted glass and hear his muted voice when he said, "I'm sorry, the office is closed." And then again, "It's closed. You'll have to come back later."

She wished Devon would come sit with her and her mother, as if he were part of their family. But he kept his distance, watching the artist finish the sketch according to Mrs. Donnor's final instructions.

"His hair was a little curlier," she said. "Not real curly, but bristly-like. Yes, that's right."

Devon thought the vice principal's input was worth as much as the secretary's, but he gave no indication of his opinion until Saavedra told Wylie to take over outside. Then he gave the detective a small smile of approval that Saavedra received graciously, which Devon was glad to see. It boded well for some degree of cooperation rather than a jealous guarding of territory that would stymie his efforts to help.

When the junior detective was outside and Tom Barrow had studied the drawing, the vice principal nodded. "Yes, that's a fair rendition."

Saavedra looked at Mrs. Amberson. "Will you come see if you know him?"

Devon watched her join the others behind the easel, noting she had been crying earlier but seemed okay now. She stared at the drawing a long time before shaking her head.

"May I look?" Amy asked.

When Saavedra lifted the drawing and turned it around, Devon recognized the man he had sat next to in the diner that morning.

Amy said in surprise, "That's Zeb's cousin!"

"Zeb who?" Saavedra asked, dread in his voice.

"Mulroney," Amy said firmly.

Remembering what Lucinda had said about the oil-rich Mulroneys, Devon could appreciate why Saavedra was frowning.

"The kid or the old man?" he asked.

"The kid," Amy said. "I used to go out with him."

"Do you know the cousin's name?"

"Zeb called him Buck."

"The last name is Powell," Mrs. Amberson said. "Isn't that right, Rene?"

The two women looked at each other with what Devon suspected was some painful history being swept under the bridge.

"Yes," the secretary answered.

Saavedra looked at Mrs. Amberson. "Any idea what he might want with your boy?"

"Oh no," Amy whimpered.

Everyone looked at her.

"It's because of me."

"How's that?" Saavedra asked.

"Zeb's mad 'cause I won't go out with him anymore."

The detective's voice was tinged with ridicule. "So you think he got his cousin to kidnap your new boyfriend?"

Amy's eyes filled with tears as she looked at Devon.

Saavedra looked at him, too. "Don'cha think that's a little far-fetched?"

Devon shrugged.

"Besides," Amy cried, "Mrs. Mulroney was in the office when I got here! Doesn't that prove Zeb's involved?"

"Gracious, I'd forgotten that," Rene Donnor said. "She came to take Zebediah out of class, but he isn't here today. She seemed confused that he wasn't, then said he must've stayed overnight with his grandparents and it must've been that Mrs. Mulroney who called in saying Li'l Zeb was sick."

Saavedra looked at Lucinda. "Would you folks mind meeting us at the police station? We'll be there directly."

Lucinda stood up and opened her purse. When she took her keys out, they jingled in the ominous quiet.

"You, too, Mrs. Amberson," Saavedra said gently. "Do you need someone to drive you?"

She shook her head, coming out from behind the counter to stand by Lucinda.

"I think it'll be best," Saavedra said, "if we let these school folks go about their business."

Marta nodded and walked out, having to duck around Detective Wylie standing guard in the door.

As they followed her, Devon told Lucinda, "I'm gonna offer to drive her."

"Good idea." Lucinda watched him catch up with Marta, then looked across at Amy. "Your blouse is a surprise."

"I finished it last night. Today's the first time I've worn it."

Lucinda didn't want to fight. "It's very pretty."

Amy gave her a brave smile, and Lucinda hugged her close as they walked.

She whispered, "Mom, will Devon find Nathan?"

"I'm sure he will. Either him or the police."

Chapter Seven

Marta studied the man driving her car as adeptly as if it were his. She had heard that Lucinda Sterling was renting her garage apartment to a good-looking man of eligible age. After watching the two of them in the school office, Marta knew they were involved beyond being landlady and tenant, and beneath her worry for Nathan she felt pleased that after all these years Lucinda might find someone to love. That thought made her long for Ben. Almost to herself, she murmured, "I wish I'd called my husband before we left."

Devon took a cell phone from his jacket pocket and handed it to her with a smile.

She thanked him and called Ben's office. While listening to the secretary say Ben was out, Marta was keenly aware of Devon. His presence beside her felt intense with understated energy, and she found herself wishing he were on the case instead of the local detectives who seemed so nonchalant about everything. Not only nonchalant, Saavedra had sounded nervous at the prospect of confronting the Mulroneys, even though their involvement was bound to be peripheral.

Marta didn't believe Amy's suggestion that jealousy was the motive for Nathan's kidnapper. Even though they were dealing with teenagers, the actual perpetrator was a man in his twenties. Surely he couldn't have acted on such a juvenile motive. She left a message for Ben, handed the phone back to Devon and shared her thoughts.

He smiled. "It's sometimes a mistake to expect criminals to be logical."

"But kidnapping is such a serious crime," she argued. "Surely this man can't have been motivated by a teenager's jealousy."

"Maybe he was paid. Doesn't Zeb come from a wealthy family?"

"Yes, but I still find it difficult to believe." She realized he hadn't been there at the beginning and had missed what she considered the most unbelievable part. "They let that man waltz in and take Nathan without showing a badge or any form of identification whatsoever!"

Devon had been pulling into the parking lot of the police station. He stopped to stare at her.

She nodded. "Incredible, isn't it? Tom watched that man handcuff Nathan before putting him in the car!" Suddenly she was crying. "Oh Lord," she moaned, hiding her face in her hands as she leaned over her lap.

Devon parked in a space, shut off the engine and pulled her close. "Go ahead and cry," he coaxed. "Take the pressure off so you can deal with what's next."

He smelled clean, as if he had just bathed and put on a fresh shirt before leaving home, and his hands were gentle holding her, his silence soothing as he cradled the weight of her grief, so she did as he said: let it all out in the strength of his embrace.

Lucinda drove into the lot with Amy and parked in a row one over from Devon and Marta. Trying not to spy on them, she nevertheless couldn't keep herself from staring.

Amy asked plaintively, "Mom, what do you think's happening to Nathan?"

Lucinda looked at her daughter's forlorn little face, the

long dark lashes over the bright blue eyes, now brimming with tears. "I don't know," she said gently. "None of this makes any sense."

"The only way it does is if Zeb's involved."

Lucinda didn't want to belittle Amy's theory, though she herself gave it little credence. Then she remembered that Amy had been right about there being a dark secret in Devon's past, and she decided if children were better than adults at figuring things out, her future looked bleak. Watching Devon and Marta in an embrace suggestive of intimacy, she told her daughter, "I hope you go to college."

"Why?" Amy asked in a baffled tone.

"So you can get a good job and support me. I'm obviously inept at understanding anything."

"Mrs. Amberson's upset and Devon's comforting her. That's all."

She looked at her daughter. "What does that have to do with anything?"

"Oh, Mom. I know you're sleeping with him."

She started to argue, then gave up. "You were right. I called the reference on his rental application and found out he left El Paso to avoid being questioned at a court of inquiry."

"About what?"

"I think I'll let him tell you."

"He's really a detective, though, isn't he?"

"He was."

"So he'll help find Nathan, won't he?"

"I'm not sure the police will want his help." She watched him get out of the car and hold the door for Marta, who slid out on the driver's side and took the keys he offered. Then they shared a smile that made Lucinda's ears burn.

"I want him to help," Amy said. "Does that count?"

Lucinda looked at her. "Of course it does. But don't say

anything when we're with the police. Let's see how they work it out among themselves."

Amy opened her door and started out.

"Amy?"

She looked back, then said with reluctance, "Okay."

When they were with the others, Lucinda forced herself to give Marta an encouraging smile. "This is awful," she murmured, hugging her. "If there's anything I can do, you'll let me know, won't you?"

Marta nodded. "Did Amy tell you they didn't even ask the man for identification?"

Lucinda looked at Devon, seeing he'd been as stunned as she by the news, then asked Marta, "How could that happen?"

"When you send your children to school," Marta said, her voice strident with anger, "there's an unspoken trust that the administration will protect them."

Amy moaned, "I hope Nathan's all right."

Before anyone could start crying, Devon said, "Let's go hear what the police have to say."

As they moved toward the building, the other two walking ahead, Devon guided Lucinda with his hand on the back of her waist. She stretched to whisper close to his ear, "Amy wants you to help the police."

He met her eyes. "I doubt I'll get much of a chance, officially."

The lobby had a marble floor and pale green walls. Facing the door was a glass display of photos depicting the department's history. To the left was a small area where a uniformed officer stood talking with a young man about retrieving his belongings from the house of a woman who had a restraining order against him. To the right of the display case, the room continued in a long rectangle, ending at a door marked NO ADMITTANCE. On the door's right was a line of gray plastic chairs, two of which were occupied by women who appeared to have been waiting a long time. Opposite them was a half-glass wall with a window allowing communication with the uniformed woman on the other side.

Her name was Crystal Chapman. Despite the uniform, she wasn't an officer but a city clerk who had gone to school with both Marta and Lucinda. She gave them a sympathetic smile and pressed a button that sounded a buzzer indicating the door marked NO ADMITTANCE had been unlocked. "Go on in," she said. "Chief Hudson is waiting for you."

Lucinda, Amy and Marta looked at Devon as if he could offer some reassuring explanation of the protocol, but all he did was open the door, then follow them through it.

A uniformed officer was waiting, a young man none of them knew. "Mrs. Amberson?"

Marta nodded.

"This way, please," he said, turning to an elevator.

They followed him inside, Marta first, then Lucinda and Amy, followed by Devon. When they got off on the second floor, they were in a large office with yellow walls and a tightly woven brown carpet muffling their footsteps. A dozen desks, each piled with paperwork and sporting a beige phone, were placed as if randomly about the room. At the end was a glass-walled office, closed for privacy with beige mini-blinds. Painted in block letters on its frosted glass door were the words: ARTHUR HUDSON, CHIEF OF POLICE. The young officer knocked, then opened the door and gestured them in.

Buck used the dirty towel to wipe off the ice pick as Zeb drove the Pontiac north toward Berrendo.

"What do you think?" Zeb asked nervously.

Buck threw the ice pick out the window, picked up the un-opened package of steak knives, and began wiping the plastic. "I think you best slow down 'fore we nab a cop 'cause you're speeding."

Zeb let off on the accelerator, checking the rearview. "I mean about Nathan."

"He won't be going anywhere soon."

Zeb laughed, a harsh nasal sound.

Buck threw the steak knives out the window, making sure he hurled them hard enough that they landed in the weeds, limp and brown from lack of rain. He picked up the pliers and began wiping them clean. "Good thing we had these. Couldn't have twisted that wire as tight without 'em."

"Good thing that wire was there," Zeb said. "We should have taken some with us."

"Next time we'll know to do that."

They looked at each other and laughed at the notion of a next time, then Buck threw the pliers into an irrigation ditch alongside the road.

"And to think we did all this without a gun," Zeb gloated. "I wouldn't have thought we could."

"I have a gun," Buck said, "but I didn't have to use it."

"Where is it?"

Buck pulled his pant leg up above his left boot and ex-tracted the snub-nosed .38 from where it had been pinching his ankle.

Zeb smiled at the sleek blue-black weapon. "Is that regis-tered?"

Buck returned the .38 to its hiding place. "I'm a felon, re-member? It's illegal for me to own a gun, so I don't guess I could register one."

"I thought about bringing one, but all of mine can be traced back to me."

"Well, like you said, we pulled it off without one. It's best when you can do that."

They drove in silence for a while, the brown mown fields slipping past on both sides of the road. Coming up on where the South Spring River emptied into the Pecos, Buck threw the towel out the window, then watched through the back as it flew on the wind before being caught on the black branch of a dead mesquite. Murmuring softly as if speaking to himself, he said, "I have dreams like what we just did."

Zeb glanced at him. "Let me know if you see anybody behind us."

Buck kept staring out the back, glancing at Zeb when he asked, "You ever have weird dreams?"

He shook his head, seeing a train coming toward them west of the road.

"I dream every night." Buck settled facing forward again. "About killing people I've never met and being in fights I can't remember. Twisting electrical wire real tight, like what we just did, I've dreamt of doing that. Where do you think all that shit comes from?"

"How should I know? They're your dreams."

"I've never yet killed anyone, so I can't figure why I dream about it all the time."

Zeb shot him a look of disbelief.

"Do you think my dreams are maybe like . . . what do you call things that predict what hasn't happened yet?"

"Predictions."

"No, there's another word. Premonitions. You think my dreams are like that?"

Zeb shrugged.

Buck saw the train slicing through the prairie. "Do you believe in reincarnation?"

"No."

The train was on top of them now, the racket of its wheels so loud Buck had to shout. "When I dream that shit, it feels like a memory of something I did so long ago it could've been in another life, or maybe they *are* premonitions and I ain't done 'em yet but will."

Zeb shouted back, "Everybody does what he wants. You may not think so, but if you didn't, you wouldn't do it. Like a girl getting raped. If she doesn't want it, there're ways to make sure it never happens. Or somebody being poor or sick or whatever. That's why I like that motto you see on cups: CARPE DIEM." He shook his fist in the air as the end of the train clattered past. "Seize the moment! Make it what you want!"

With only the wind whipping past the open windows, Buck thought about Zeb's life. "I feel more like I get seized."

Zeb looked at him sideways.

"Like when I robbed that Quick Stop. I didn't plan to do that. I sure didn't grow up thinking someday I'd be a thief. One day I just needed money real bad and it seemed the fastest way to get some. It was what you call a split-second decision that locked in the next five years of my life, 'cause I got caught and sent to prison and then was on parole and all. And like what we just did. All I wanted was a ride home from Albuquerque. Wasn't any of my doing that you were the one to pick me up. But while we were driving down here, we hatched this plan, and now we're tighter'n we've ever been. Ain't that how you feel, Zeb?"

"Yeah, sure."

"When you agreed to pick me up at the airport, did you know what we'd be planning on the trip back?"

"Not exactly, but I knew I'd do something. It was when we were talking about it that the plan came clear, but I started out with a strong intention."

"My only intention was to go home." Buck looked behind them again. Far in the distance he could see the red light on the end of the train like a tiny prick of blood under the blue sky.

"That's where you're going now."

"Is it?" he asked, not having considered what came next.

"After you drop me off, you can drive down to Carlsbad or maybe even all the way to El Paso and sell this car. The registration's in the glove box there." He nodded at it as if Buck didn't know where the glove compartment was. "You can use the money to buy another car, then you'll be home with wheels all your own. That's a helluva lot more than you had when you got off that plane in Albuquerque."

Buck wiped at a speck of blood on the front of his shirt, but it had already dried into what he guessed was a perfect circle of guilt. "What about the rest of our story? I mean about what we were doing together."

"I've been sick in bed all day. I don't know what you were doing. That's for you to decide. But don't tell me because I don't know, understand?"

He nodded. "So we weren't together and don't have any idea what the other was doing."

"That's right."

"Think I'll sell the car in Juárez. Won't nobody look for it there."

"Now you're thinking smart."

Buck slid lower on his tailbone, trying to feel better about himself. Zeb was the most intelligent person he knew, so if Zeb thought he was smart, he must be. But Buck still couldn't shake the uneasiness he felt. "I wish it was dark already. I'm gonna be a sitting duck driving around in this car."

"They probably don't even know Nathan's missing yet."

Buck hadn't told Zeb the school secretary had called the

kid's mother to say she could pick him up in an hour. Since that hour was long gone, he was pretty sure the *they* who knew included the cops. He reasoned he would be okay as soon as he got rid of the car. In the meantime, though, he and Zeb were driving back into enemy territory a good four hours before sunset.

Chapter Eight

After her unsuccessful run on her son's bank account, Alicia sat sipping Dubonnet as she stared at a photograph of herself kept on the parson's table behind the gold damask sofa in her sunlit living room. The photo she treasured as a portrait of denied promise had been taken while she was perched on the top rail of a corral at her parents' ranch in the hill country of Texas. She had been eighteen, her slender body clothed in tight jeans and a sleeveless yellow blouse, a brown cowboy hat riding her golden curls, her smile radiating from a young woman whom everyone had believed would marry well and live happily. Everyone had been wrong.

Beyond being shackled to an unhappy husband in an inadequate town, Alicia had soon discovered her father-in-law was so opposed to her marriage that he disowned her husband. The public notice printed in the local newspaper deprived Silas not only of his patrimony, but also the gumption to make it on his own somewhere else.

Although Old Zeb showed no inclination toward retracting the announcement, he did develop a pernicious fondness for Alicia. His lavish gifts were bribes to keep her in the family so her ascendancy in his good graces would further aggravate his son's punishment. Alicia was cooperative. When *her* son was born, she named him Zebediah Mulroney II rather than Silas Junior, thereby pitting him, too, against the man in the middle. As Li'l Zeb grew, favored as his grandfather's heir, Silas reacted by blaming the boy. Any infraction was deemed cause for punishment. And just as in his own youth date rape had been euphemistically considered merely rambunctious, he referred to his son's punishment as spankings when in reality they were brutal beatings delivered with a belt.

Because Alicia often shared the initial curve of the cycle, she knew the sessions always followed a bout of serious drinking. Early in those evenings she was cheerfully gay, deflecting his animosity by being entertaining, but as the night progressed and he became sullen, she found a way to escape. That was when he went looking for Zeb. Alicia sat in her room, a telephone within reach but her hands idle, her will concentrated on the lock securing her door against her husband. Even after it was over, she sat immobile, afraid to venture out. Only at dawn did she feel safe enough to comfort her son. Whimpering as if in horrified discovery, she untied the restraints, soothed his welts with a cooling salve, and helped him drink a cup of hot chocolate laced with cognac. When the time came, she called from the bedside phone to say Zebediah was ill and wouldn't be in school that day, then she slid under the covers and cradled him with the love so severely lacking in their lives.

She now realized she had created a masochist by rewarding him for having been punished, just as Silas had created a sadist who craved to give back what had been given. Neither of them was motivated by the child's well-being, only a need to find compensation for their own disappointments. Sitting in her living room contemplating the portrait of herself in her last summer of promise, Alicia felt deeply afraid. When she heard someone enter the foyer, she waited without breathing to see who would come in.

It was Li'l Zeb. His black clothes met the school's dress code, but she suspected it was another uniform he aspired to emulate: that of the storm trooper, the terrorist, the instigator of chaos. He stopped on the threshold and asked, "What's wrong?"

She smiled bitterly, thinking the inquisitor was perceptive. "I went to the school looking for you."

He shrugged. "Gram called in for me."

"Did she see you leave?"

"Not till just now. I've been sick in bed all day."

On the parson's table was a small crystal swan. She picked it up and threw it. He ducked and the bird hit the wall. As if it hadn't happened and the crystal wasn't now shards on the floor, she said calmly, "Amy Sterling's boyfriend is missing. You remember Amy, don't you? The girl whose photographs fill that album you keep with your dirty movies?"

He stood up straight, his baffled expression hardening into a sneer. "What were you doing in my stuff?"

"Looking for your bankbook."

His sneer gave way to curiosity. "Do you need money?"

"Do you think your father gives me any?"

"I guess not."

"Your grandfather?"

"He probably would if you asked."

She shook her head. "He wants me here. It's part of his revenge, to spoil me as an added torture for your father. But what you've just done puts torture in a whole new class."

He frowned. "What're you talking about?"

"Nathan Wheeler. Have you forgotten him already?"

"I don't know him."

She stood up and crossed to the highboy. Refilling her glass, she teased, "What about Cousin Buck? Does he know Nathan?" When she turned back around, she winced at how pathetic he looked. "You'd better learn to control your expressions, Zeb. I expect the police will be here soon."

"Why?"

"Nathan Wheeler is missing."

"What's that got to do with me?"

"Perhaps nothing, as long as no one else sees your pictures of Amy. But if the police come and search your room, being as it's her boyfriend who's missing, I suspect those photographs might be useful in court."

He looked over his shoulder at the curving staircase.

"Yes, you should get rid of them. But I suggest you don't leave the house, since you're supposed to be sick."

He turned toward the stairs.

"By the way," she called, stopping him on the first step, "What did your grandmother say is wrong with you? I should know in case anyone asks."

"I have a stomachache," he said, looking as if it were true.

"Too bad," she crooned. "Maybe I should give you an enema."

"You try and I'll give you one!"

She laughed, watching him stalk up the stairs.

Forty miles south of the Mulroney estate, Buck Powell was also walking up a flight of stairs, but the steps under his feet were steel and only three were required to ascend from the dirt of his parents' front yard to the door of their trailer. Although he technically didn't live there anymore, he didn't knock, figuring since he had a key it would be silly.

His mother was watching television from where she sat on an orange-and-yellow plaid sofa that had been a mistake direct from the showroom. After ten years of hard wear, it was an eyesore. Immense for a trailer, the sofa took up half the floor space when its two ends were reclined, which they almost always were since his parents were habitually sprawled in front of the TV. Their occupation of the sofa was the only evidence he had seen that they possessed a nesting instinct.

His mother's brown braid had been cut since the last time he was home. Now her hair fell in wispy curls around her neck as she watched him through puffy dark eyes. Mostly licked off, her lipstick resembled the yellowed brown of a squashed apple, and sometime earlier in the day she had shadowed her eyes with purple smudges that almost imitated the heroin look he had seen on the high school girls. He went into the kitchen and opened the refrigerator. Inside he found a liter of Sam's Cola.

He carried the plastic bottle over to the chair that sat catty-corner to his mother's reclined end of the sofa, perched on the chair's edge and twisted the cap open with a hiss of escaping carbonation. As he guzzled the cola straight from the bottle, he joined his mother in watching Oprah berate her audience for not living up to their peak performance. "Why not?" she kept asking. When a woman said her treadmill collected dust in the basement, Oprah asked in a bewildered tone, "Why?" Buck belched into her painted face just before she turned her back on the camera, which made him laugh, and that finally inspired his mother to speak.

"Don't drink all your dad's soda."

He set the open bottle on the floor and leaned back fiddling with the cap. "Ain't you gonna say you're glad to see me?"

"Did you get a job up north?"

All he had done in Denver was wander between the bus station's coffee shop and his fleabag hotel, shivering in his quilted jacket that had been adequate in Artesia but sadly thin in the Rockies. When summer came, he made the same rounds sweating under the layers of smog suffocating the city. "They all called me over-qualified for what they were offering."

Her eyes narrowed with suspicion. "So where'd you get the cash for your ticket home?"

"Won it at a casino."

"How much'd you win?"

"Two hundred twelve dollars. My ticket was one-ninety-five."

She looked back at Oprah. "Your dad'll be home soon and want his soda cold."

He studied her mule slippers that had once been pink but were now a tattered gray, her pudgy hands limp in the lap of her purple sweatpants, her breasts sagging beneath her faded blue sweatshirt, the folds of fat in her cheeks. "Why did you and Dad have me?"

She let her gaze wander over to him. "Guess we was hoping for someone to take care of us in our old age."

She looked back at Oprah, who was talking to Harrison Ford, an actor paid millions for every movie he made. Buck asked, "You like that guy?"

She shrugged.

He guessed Harrison Ford was an okay actor, along the lines of John Wayne who always played himself, but he liked the guys who changed into different people for each movie. That was acting in his opinion, though no one ever asked. If they had, he would have said none of those Hollywood guys deserved all the money they got. Millions to buy ranches and islands and private jets, while people like his parents lived in trailers on the desert without enough money to get the cooler fixed. Last fall, when the temperature inside hit a hundred and twenty by late afternoon and didn't start dropping till bedtime, and even then the back rooms stayed sultry with steam from the kitchen, was when Buck had decided Denver sounded pretty good.

It was also when his parole had been up so he could go wherever without asking. His dad had said anybody could get a job in Denver, and his mom said nothing ever came to a person who didn't try, so he'd left knowing he wouldn't be missed. Now he was home after being gone nine months, the same amount of time he had lived inside his mother's body, though thinking about that made him feel queasy.

He put the soda back in the refrigerator and closed the door, then stared out the window above the sink. The prairie seemed flat all the way to the mountains, but he knew in between were canyons and ridges invisible from a distance. Sometimes he wished he were a toad or a snake living out there, a camouflaged creature difficult to see even up close. If he were a snake, he would stay away from people. Horses, too. They killed snakes, rearing up and stomping them to death with their hooves. Buck had seen it happen. Nobody liked snakes, so he didn't guess he would lose much by being one.

The clunk of a truck running on five cylinders came into the yard and died without being shut off. Buck hurried into the bathroom, wanting to straighten up before seeing his father, though when he looked into the mirror there wasn't much he could do. His hair was short and bristly so didn't need combing. His face was clean. The specks of dried blood on the front of his shirt could be anything—ketchup, mud, chocolate pudding for that matter.

From beyond the door, he heard his father's gruff voice: "Whose car is that?"

"Buck's," his mother said, the dearth of warmth in her voice saying he had come home empty-handed.

He listened to his father trundle by in the hall, then slid the door open and looked down toward the bedrooms. Hearing his father move around and feeling the shift of weight on the floor, he returned to the living room and sat down in the chair to watch Oprah as if he had been there all along. The beautiful talk show host in diamond earrings was gushing all over the millionaire actor in starched jeans as if they both belonged to the same country club.

"I wonder if she knows," he said, "how many sad-ass housewives watch her show drunk everyday."

"I ain't drinking," Berta whispered. "Don't go putting ideas in your dad's head!"

Which told Buck his mother was one of those sad-ass housewives. He almost smiled, knowing next time he wanted vodka he could find a bottle hidden in the trailer, but just then his father came into the kitchen and opened the refrigerator. "Who drank my soda?" he barked, killing Buck's smile. He stood up when his father slammed the door and faced him across the breakfast bar behind the couch.

Eldon Powell was as gray as the work clothes he wore for his job at the junkyard. His body was tight and wiry, the veins on his hands like ridges of corduroy, his heavy beard stubbling his cheeks like tombstones in a cemetery for gnats. "You get a job?"

Buck shook his head.

Berta brushed past him on her way to the kitchen. She took out the plastic jug and set it on the counter, then filled a tumbler with ice cubes and poured cola over the top. The hiss of carbonation was the only sound other than a commercial advertising pantyhose. The announcer said if you wore Hanes, men would thank their lucky stars you were wearing a skirt.

Buck stepped out of the way as Eldon moved to the sofa and kicked back in the recliner. Berta handed him the glass of cola and a bowl of peanuts still in the shell. He nestled the bowl in his lap, took a long drink of the cola and set the glass down, then picked up the remote and switched to a wrestling match. After cracking and munching a few peanuts, he asked, "How was Denver?"

Buck sat back down. "Cold in winter, smoggy in summer."

"What'd you expect?"

"Didn't have no expectations. Went there to find out."

Eldon's dark eyes pinned him. "You don't have expectations, how's anything gonna happen?"

"Things happen whether you expect 'em or not."

"Did'ya hear what he said?" Eldon shouted over his shoulder.

"I heard," Berta answered, not looking up from the onion she was chopping.

He glowered at Buck. "You expect nothing, that's what you get." He stared a moment longer, as if giving time for his wisdom to sink in, then looked back at the wrestlers.

Buck muttered, "I guess you expected a lot less than Ol' Zeb Mulroney."

Eldon spit a peanut into the bowl. "Zeb stole what was ours! Your great grandpa split the land even 'tween Zeb's dad and my ma. Was Zeb's dad bought the mineral rights out from under my dad. Left him with only water 'cause he wanted to be a rancher. Went under in the drought and had to sell, but the new owners didn't get the mineral rights 'cause Zeb had 'em. You think he shared when he found oil? No sir! It'd be half ours if Zeb'd done right."

Buck had heard it before. "My point is, your expectations didn't match what you got."

"They would've if Zeb'd been fair!"

"This land'd still belong to the Apaches if life was fair."

"I'd fight alongside 'em if it'd mean taking it away from the Mulroneys!"

"Now, Eldon," Berta soothed from the kitchen. "You're gonna give yourself 'nother heart attack."

He made a noise like spitting, then muttered at the wrestlers, "Beat the shit outta the sonofabitch!"

Buck slumped in his chair. He had supposed that after the better part of a year his parents might have something new to say. "Guess not," he mumbled, standing up.

"You're not staying for supper?" Berta asked, holding a package of ground beef she was about to thaw in the micro-wave.

"I don't remember being invited."

She opened her mouth but kept quiet, staring as if he were crazy.

"You buy that Pontiac in Denver?" Eldon asked.

Buck frowned that his father had taken enough notice of the car to remember its make. "Why do you say that?"

"It's got Colorado plates! D'ya think I'm blind?"

"It ain't mine," Buck said, resenting his tone. "B'longs to a friend."

"Guess your friend ain't got any more money'n you do to drive a junker like that."

"Look who's talking! Your truck ain't exactly a prize."

"It's a classic!" He kicked his footrest down and sat up straight, glaring over the bowl of peanuts in his lap. "May need a little engine work, but the body's perfect!"

"Go on, if you're leaving," Berta yelled. "You'll give him a heart attack, you get him going 'bout that truck!"

Buck walked out and slammed the door. He hoped one of them would follow and plead with him to stay for supper, but all he heard were his own footsteps crunching the desert gravel. Stabbing himself behind the wheel, he turned the Pontiac's ignition, then threw sand against the back of his father's '63 Chevy as he tore out of the yard. The pickup's license plate in his rearview mirror made him realize the combination of the station wagon's Colorado plates and his own recent return from Denver would point a finger hard to ignore. He wondered if Zeb had thought of that, then decided his cousin wasn't savvy enough to be so far ahead of the game.

When he saw a trailer that looked empty despite having a Ford Mustang nearby, he stopped and knocked on the door, planning to act lost if someone opened it. No one did, so he set about swapping license plates, even going so far as to smear the Colorado plate with dust so maybe the Mustang's owner wouldn't notice anytime soon.

Back on the highway, he felt so pleased with himself he decided a couple of beers would top him off just right for the long drive to El Paso. He pulled into the parking lot of the first tavern he saw, a low cinderblock building called The Bat's Cave. As he walked inside, he chuckled, thinking Nathan Wheeler would no doubt relish a beer about now.

Chapter Nine

Devon was sitting at the kitchen table watching Amy take cups from the cabinet. Her long black hair slid back and forth across the slippery silk of her blouse with a whispered sound that made him think of girls sharing secrets. When she set a cup and saucer in front of him, then leaned slightly forward as she filled the cup with coffee, the décolletage of her blouse was close enough for him to kiss without a whole lot of effort. He didn't deny himself the pleasure of caressing her with his eyes—there were few sights more beautiful in his estimation than a young woman's breasts—but he sincerely wished she would change her blouse.

As she filled her mother's cup, then her own, returned the pot and went to the refrigerator for milk, he and Lucinda watched each other over the banal terrain of the kitchen table, knowing they were contemplating a quest the culmination of which in all likelihood would strike a severe blow at Amy.

She returned with the carton of milk, sat down and poured a generous amount in her coffee, then slowly stirred it in a hypnotic rhythm. Realizing they were watching, she glanced back and forth between them before she laid her spoon in her saucer and folded her hands in her lap. "So?"

He realized how much aversion he had accumulated in his months off the job by how much energy it was taking to overcome his inertia and force his mind into gear. He thought of his gun, knowing he would need it to confront the man he had sat next to in Denny's, also knowing a manhunt was no place for an ex-cop who had lost the edge of his moral superiority over criminals by becoming one, even less a place for such a man to take a woman and child. Considering all that, he gave Amy what he hoped was an encouraging smile and asked, "You recognized the man in the police sketch?"

She nodded.

"From where?"

"I saw him with Zeb last fall."

In the professional voice he had developed over the years to soften up witnesses, a gently entreating tone he hadn't used for a while, he said, "Tell me about it."

"Zeb and I were at the Sonic on South Main on a Saturday night. We'd been to the movies and had gone for a Coke and to just hang out, you know. Zeb has a sports car now, but then he had a Jeep Cherokee his grandfather had given him. When Buck came over, Zeb let him in the back seat." She glanced at her mother, then looked at him again. "Buck was, I don't know, like unhappy, you know?"

"What about?"

"He said he had just gotten off parole, but now that he was free to do anything he wanted, he felt lost on his own."

"What'd he go to prison for?"

It was Lucinda who said, "He robbed a convenience store."

"Did he use a gun?"

"I believe so."

"Was anyone hurt?"

"I don't think so."

"What'd he serve? A coupla years?"

They both shrugged. He smiled. "Okay. So now he's off parole and looking for something to do. What's his cousin Zeb like?"

Amy and Lucinda looked at each other as if waiting for the other to answer first, then said in unison, "I didn't like him."

Devon laughed. "Well, that's unanimous. What's wrong with him?"

"He's stuck-up," Amy said. "Thinks he's hot shit when he's really a turd."

Lucinda stared at her daughter, then laughed. "That's an accurate, if scatological, description."

"What's scatological mean?" Amy asked.

"Look it up."

While she was in her room doing that, Lucinda told Devon about the incident in the theater when Zeb had hurt Joe Mason so badly he was taken to the hospital in an ambulance. Devon winced at the story, knowing it didn't bode well for Nathan's fate.

Amy came back and plunked herself into her chair. "Preoccupied with obscenity," she announced, "but it only comes to mind when I think of Zeb."

"In the school office," Devon said, "you thought he was motivated by jealousy. You still think that?"

"I know it sounds egotistical," she said, "but Zeb's been weird ever since I started dating Nathan. He hangs around on the edge of everything and watches with this really sour face. When I broke up with him he acted like he didn't care, and I didn't think he did till I started dating Nathan. Then all of a sudden it was like Zeb was everywhere. Every time I turned around he was staring at me in this really creepy way. Nathan said Zeb did it to him, too. So when I saw that it was Zeb's cousin who took Nathan out of school, I just immediately thought he did it for Zeb."

Devon tried to imagine the scenario, but kept coming back to how Buck could expect to get away with it. One answer was that maybe he was so lost on the outside he was looking for a ticket back. If that turned out to be true, it might mean Nathan had a good chance to survive unless Buck overplayed his hand. Murder on top of kidnapping was a capital crime in every state with a death penalty, which included New Mexico. "Do you have any idea where they might have taken Nathan?"

Amy shook her head.

"How about where Buck lives?"

"No," she said.

Lucinda left the table and came back with the phone book. After thumbing through several pages, she looked up and said, "His parents live on Atoka Road in Artesia."

She and Amy both watched him, their faces hopeful.

"The chief of police made it pretty clear he wants me to stay out of this."

"What'll he do if you don't?" Amy asked.

"Depends on how far I go."

"Can he arrest you?" Lucinda asked.

"Maybe."

"For just asking a few questions?" Amy prodded.

"Sometimes the wrong person asking questions can tumble an investigation like a wheelbarrow of apples."

Lucinda smiled, but Amy was adamant. "This is a free country," she said as if that were new information. "We have the right to talk to whoever we want."

He smiled. "Do I need to tell you about yelling 'Fire' in a crowded theater?"

"No, I've heard that," she huffed. "But we can't just sit and do nothing!"

"Someone should be here to answer the phone," he countered, looking at Lucinda, who seemed to agree.

"Don't make me stay here alone!" Amy pleaded.

Lucinda promised, "I won't do that, Amy."

They both looked at him. Though he knew any progress he made would most likely be on his own, he decided maybe it was enough that they kept Amy occupied so her imagination didn't make things worse than they were. "All right. We'll go together and do what we can."

She smiled her gratitude.

"One condition," he told her.

"What?"

He let his eyes go where they shouldn't, then met hers with a smile when he said, "I want you to change clothes."

Lucinda watched her leave, then looked at him.

He stood up and tucked his chair under the table. "It's apt to get cold after dark, so you best bring some jackets."

He crossed the shadowed back yard, already somber with dusk. Inside his room, he took off his jacket and tossed it on the sofa, then opened his dresser for the 9mm Beretta hidden beneath his loose socks. As he shrugged into the holster, he knew if things fell in such a way that he had to use the gun, he'd have a hard time explaining having taken the women along.

Lucinda stood in the open door of her daughter's room and watched Amy pull on a black sweatshirt with the red Coyote mascot howling on the front. She wished the school colors weren't red and black. They seemed mean somehow, and she thought high school should be a tender time of gentle kindness. Not that it ever was, she scoffed, remembering the thousand emotional crises that seemed to happen every day in a teenager's life. Still, she wanted for Amy so many of the things she herself hadn't known despite being raised by two parents. But her parents had been largely absent from her life—too old to participate or understand what she felt—and Lucinda wanted to shelter Amy from the loneliness she had known.

Looking around the room, she noted that the blue flow-ered comforter she had bought two Christmases ago for Amy's single bed was wearing well. On the wall above the white rattan headboard, posters of Jakob Dylan and Kurt Cobain were centerpieces surrounded by a collage of smaller pictures of musicians and actors cut from magazines. A black boom box squatted on the bedside table along with its tower of CDs, most of which Lucinda would have to be bribed to listen to. On one wall was a natural pine bookcase whose shelves were filled with Beanie Babies, an aquarium housing a *Star Wars* landscape, a collection of makeup more vast than her own and at the top, no doubt forgotten, a few paperbacks by V. C. Andrews and Stephen King gathering dust. The oak floor beside the bed was covered with a fringed rug matching the comforter—finding that precise shade of blue had been no mean feat—and the curtains were coordinated in stripes of sky and cobalt blue, striking an ominous resonance off the eyes of Jakob and Kurt peering as if omnisciently down from the walls. Lucinda shivered, remembering that one of those boys was dead, the blond one who had grown up without a fa-mous father to teach him the ropes of celebrity, maybe without any father for all she knew, maybe like Nathan, a boy on his own far too young.

She wanted to tell Amy not to mourn Nathan if it turned out he didn't survive whatever was happening, not to let his misfortune mar her youth; but to have that wish granted would make Amy callous, something Lucinda wanted even less than to see her hurt. Realizing there was no way Amy could skate free in the days ahead, Lucinda wanted to hug her close, to soothe away the tears that hadn't yet come, maybe to stop them at their source and prevent the pain that caused them. But she could do none of that, not even hug her, be-cause Amy was leaning to the side as she brushed her long black hair with the energy of impending action, optimistic with the prospect of helping a boy who was caught in a maelstrom beyond anyone's reckoning, and not for heaven itself would Lucinda have destroyed Amy's faith that she could make a difference in what lay ahead. Yet when Amy looked up, Lucinda guessed the expression on her face did shake that faith.

"Mom," she asked, "Nathan's gonna be okay, you believe that, don't you?"

She forced herself to sound more confident than she felt. "I'm sure of it, but he's probably scared, so the sooner we find him the better."

Sitting in the middle of the bench seat in Devon's old truck, Amy thought this must be what it felt like to have two parents, one on each side whenever they went somewhere as a family. She wished Devon *had* been her father. He seemed so strong and safe, but then she guessed she didn't really know him all that well. She looked at her mother, who gave her a fragile smile, making her long for him to love them, to cherish and protect them in the way of husbands and fathers. Impulsively she asked, "Does life ever turn out the way we want?"

She felt the adults look at each other, but she stared straight ahead, embarrassed by the childishness of her question.

Her mother answered it. "I have you."

Amy knew the story of the untimely death of her father, so she didn't guess the initial news of her conception had been cause for celebration. But then nothing would be, coming so soon after losing a loved one. Having already lost two of her grandparents, she didn't want to mourn Nathan. Her mother had said he was probably no more than scared, and she wanted to believe her, and that they were now searching for him merely because he was lost. But when Devon turned south on the Old Dexter Highway, the sudden change of wind through the open windows lifted the side of his jacket enough that she saw the grip of a pistol beneath his arm. The gun convinced her Nathan was in serious trouble. Devon glanced at her as he shifted gears, and in his eyes she saw a depth of concern that increased her fear.

She argued that he was a cop and therefore accustomed to bad scenarios. Not only a cop, a homicide detective, so of course he would expect the worst. But this wasn't El Paso. Murders must be as common there as traffic tickets. She tried to remember the last one she had heard of in Berrendo. It had been when Emilia Pacheco's father shot and killed her mother's lover. Amy had been only fourteen, and it had been a scandal the grownups wouldn't discuss in front of children.

She looked at Devon again, wondering if he had ever killed anyone in the line of duty. She also wondered what he would do if he found his wife with another man. That made her wonder why someone his age wasn't married, if he was divorced or maybe a widower, which led her back to thinking of her father. If Lyle Sterling had married her mother before he died, Lucinda would have been a widow all these years instead of an unwed mother. Amy wondered if the capacity to lose men was hereditary. When she again looked at her mother, Lucinda gave her another fragile smile, and Amy realized both her mother and Devon were most concerned about her, which meant they thought Nathan was beyond help.

She closed her eyes and concentrated on trying to imagine where he was. Above the hum of tires and drone of the engine, she heard water dripping. Her eyes sprang open and she looked around to make certain it hadn't suddenly started raining. The sky was darkening with dusk but there wasn't a cloud anywhere. Neither could she spot any evidence of leaking under the dash. She considered telling her mother and Devon about the water, but when she closed her eyes and tried to retrieve the sound, she heard only the truck and the wind of its passing.

Under a canopy of ancient cottonwoods, the white sign for the South Spring Ranch glowed by the side of the road. In small gold letters near the bottom the sign read: *Established 1874*. Abruptly she asked Devon, "Did you know John Chisum started that ranch?"

He nodded.

"Chisum was famous for his jinglebob brand," she continued, assuming his ignorance because she needed to talk, "but you know what that was? He sliced half the cow's ear nearly off, so it hung down like a flap. That made it easy to pick his cattle out of a herd when lots of different brands were mixed together, so at first the idea seems really smart, but when you think about it you realize how cruel he was to inflict that pain on all those cows just for his convenience."

Devon looked across at her mother.

"What?" Amy asked. "Am I talking too much?"

"No, sweetheart," her mother said.

She looked back and forth between them. "You're humoring me, aren't you? You're afraid I'll become hysterical or something. That I'll make some connection with how cruel John Chisum was to how mean Buck Powell is to have taken Nathan and be holding him somewhere. But they wouldn't just hold him, would they? They're doing things to him, aren't they? Beating him up? Is that what you think they're doing?"

"I'm sure they're not," her mother said firmly.

"What do you think, Devon?" she demanded. "They're hurting him, maybe right this very minute, aren't they!"

He glanced at her but didn't answer.

"Tell me!" she shouted.

"Amy," her mother warned.

She ignored her. "I want to know what you really think, not what I should hear or can handle!"

Softly Devon said, "I don't know what they're doing to him. Whatever I say will be a guess, and I try not to do that."

"Why?"

"I don't have enough information. Guesses pulled out of thin air lead to speculations that might take us away from the truth instead of toward it."

She took a deep breath and let it out slowly.

"In the beginning of an investigation," he said, "it's important not to jump to conclusions. There's always a temptation to do that, because the mind likes things neat, but a lot of life is chaotic, and sometimes you have to let the chaos be while you pick your way through it, following a thread until you find another it ties into. Then maybe you can begin to discern a pattern, and from there you can extrapolate, which is a kind of guessing, but by then you've got something to go on, you haven't just pulled it out of thin air. Then, too, is when instinct comes into play. Sometimes, with just a few pieces of information, you can intuit the truth. That takes a good bit of experience, though, or maybe psychic ability." He paused to smile. "Right now we're at square one, and it's best not to track ourselves toward any particular solution."

"Just let the chaos be," she murmured.

"That's what we're doing," he agreed.

Again she considered telling them she had heard water dripping when she tried to imagine Nathan's location, but she decided to keep quiet in case what she had experienced turned out to be that psychic ability Devon had said would be useful when they had more facts. She smiled at her mother, then looked straight ahead, reassured by the rationality of a detective's approach.

Having thrown up the only meal he'd had in the last twenty-four hours, Pete Reck was feeling dizzy as he approached the librarian's house. The sky was mauve with the last of sunset when he rang her doorbell. Inside he could hear the chime followed by silence. He rang it again, thinking he had to get something to eat before trekking north on 285 in the hope of catching a ride to I-40. Maybe when he told Lucinda Sterling what he had come here to say, she would invite him into her kitchen and cook him a meal. He rang the bell again, eager to have his fantasy fulfilled.

The yellow house was silent, not even a light inside to fight the deepening shadows of dusk. Pete took a few steps back and looked at the dark front windows, rebuking himself for thinking something was possible merely because he wanted it to happen. Still in all, he had come here on a mission of gratitude. It didn't seem right that the fates denied him the satisfaction of delivering praise.

He followed the driveway past the chimney to a white picket fence running from the house to a corner of the garage. Outside the fence he stopped and looked at the smooth expanse of mown lawn, still green despite the yellowing leaves of the huge mulberry in the center of the yard. A brick walk led from the back of the house to a door in the side of the garage. Pete opened the gate in the picket fence and left it ajar so he could get out fast if he needed to, then walked to the wide side of the garage and peered in through a window.

He was surprised to see an apartment, just one room but a place perfect for him. He could see a cubbyhole kitchen and a door that probably led to a bathroom. There was a weight bench, too, as if everything was all set up for him to move in. Then he realized the room was already occupied, no doubt by a man, and he wondered how the resident was related to the librarian, if he was a brother or uncle or what. Maybe he was the one Lucinda took behind the curtains Pete imagined would be on her bed. Maybe they did those things married people did, the things he had heard his parents do in the dead of night and seen countless couples perform on screens in darkened theaters when he still lived at home and was given money to spend on things like movies, though his parents hadn't suspected what kind he liked.

He heard a car door open, then a nasal voice through the static of a walkie-talkie. A quick glance toward the alley revealed an adobe wall too high to jump. Given time he could climb it, but the cop was already coming through the picket gate. He was a slight man, shorter than Pete but carrying more weight. His uniform was brown, the leather of his gun belt black like his shoes, the metal buckle catching light from the streetlamp that had just now come on at the end of the alley.

"What'cha doing?" he asked.

When Pete gave no answer, the cop asked, "You live here?"

Pete shook his head.

"What'cha doing here then?"

"Just looking," Pete said, as if he were window-shopping in a department store.

"You want to put your pack down?" the cop suggested. Then warned, "Keep your hands where I can see 'em."

Pete shrugged his pack off his shoulders and let it fall. He stepped away from it, holding his hands clear of his body, having been taught the drill by cops far rougher than the one facing him now had so far proved to be.

"You got any weapons?"

Pete shook his head.

"Face the fence and lean on it with your hands so I can find out."

Pete did and was frisked, the cop's pat down fast and efficient.

"Okay," he said. "Stand up. Hands behind your back."

As the cuffs were locked on his wrists, Pete asked, "Can I get my pack?"

"I'll come back for it after you're in the car." He took hold of Pete's arm and propelled him through the gate and down the driveway to the white squad car at the curb.

Pete searched every window of every house but couldn't spot the face of whoever had turned him in. Over his shoulder, he asked, "They serve supper yet in lockup?"

The cop shook his head.

"What're they having tonight?"

"Hot dogs and beans," the cop said, opening the back door of his car.

Pete grimaced as he got in, still tasting wieners every time he burped.

The cop closed the door, then said into the walkie-talkie pinned to his epaulet, "I've got him. Ten-four."

Chapter Ten

Through binoculars, Alicia Mulroney watched the car advance along the edge of the pecan grove toward her front yard. The grove was dark, the leaves just beginning to change, not with any semblance of color but merely withering. On the other side of the driveway was a field of tall grasses, yellow in the sunset. The sedan was beige. In its front seat were two men, no doubt the detectives who had earlier accompanied Marta Amberson into the school's office. Reassuring herself that they hadn't appeared to be the least bit intimidating, Alicia hid the binoculars behind a pillow on the sofa and walked over to the highboy to refill her glass with Dubonnet.

As nearly as she could remember, this was her fifth, but the liqueur was an aperitif and she assumed it wasn't highly alcoholic. In any case, she felt confident that her wits were sharp enough to deal with the buffoons about to enter her home. Carrying her drink, she walked over to the white phone on a table at one end of her sofa, picked up the receiver and, using a finger on the same hand, pressed the intercom to ring the phone in Zeb's room. She waited for him to answer as she watched the sedan pass through the open gate in the black wrought iron fence surrounding her yard.

Zeb, too, was watching the car. As he listened to his telephone ring, he had to fight a sensation of dread. His mother had been right about the pictures of Amy. He should have thrown them out before, and he wondered what else he may have overlooked. Conceding his mother might be a valuable ally, he finally moved across the room and picked up the phone.

Alicia smiled, hearing him breathe at the other end of the line. "The police are here. Shall I say you're too sick to be disturbed?"

He considered agreeing to that ploy, but it would only be a stall and he wanted to know what attitude the cops were taking. "I'll be down," he said, then carefully replaced the receiver as if his finesse in such a small detail mattered. On impulse he called the office of his grandfather's attorney.

His call was put through without delay, and the crusty voice of Ambrose Scott was soon asking after Zeb's health.

"I'm fine," he answered. "Just curious about a point of law, is all."

"I'll be happy to answer any question you have," Scott replied magnanimously.

"If the police come to someone's home to question him about a possible crime," Zeb said in a near whisper, "they need a warrant before they can search the house, don't they?"

There was a long pause before Scott said, "Yes, that's certainly true."

"And they have to have a good reason to get a warrant, right?"

"Sufficient reason to convince a judge, yes."

"And even if they had a warrant, could a person stall until his attorney had a chance to get there?"

"I'm not sure, not being a criminal lawyer, but it would certainly be worth a try. Are you having a problem with the police, Zeb?"

"No, I was just curious. Thanks for your time."

He hung up, then quickly stripped himself naked and stuffed everything into the hamper in his bathroom. He had worn the clothes only a few minutes, having taken two complete sets when he went to his grandparents' the night before. The clothes he had worn at the cemetery, and then later, the red polo shirt and black slacks, were wadded in a box in his grandparents' attic. No matter what shook down from here, Zeb didn't figure any cop would have the nerve to search Old Zeb's house, not if he valued his job. He laughed as he stepped into gray silk pajamas. He received a new pair from his grandmother every Christmas, but this would be the first time he had worn pajamas since he turned thirteen.

Downstairs in the living room, Alicia tucked her empty glass into a cubbyhole in the highboy when she heard the doorbell ring. She closed the liquor cabinet and sat down on the sofa, picked up the latest catalogue from Neiman Marcus, and was flipping through its pages when she heard the maid come in.

A middle-aged dark Hispanic, Lupe waited for Alicia to look up before she said apologetically, "*Señora,* two policemen are asking to speak with you."

Alicia pretended surprise. "Whatever for?"

"I don't know, *señora.*"

After holding the maid's eyes for a moment of feigned astonishment, she said sprightly, "Show them in."

She held the catalogue as if forgotten on her lap, the page deliberately left open to a display of jewelry, each piece of which cost more than what she supposed the average policeman's annual salary to be. The detectives stopped just inside the door, too far away to appreciate her intended snub. With a sniff of disappointment, she laid the catalogue on the table in front of her and rose to her feet.

"Gentlemen," she said, smiling graciously, "please come in."

"We're sorry to bother you, Mrs. Mulroney," the slim-hipped, dark one said. "Maybe you remember us from when we investigated a burglary here a few months back?"

She kept her face blank, pretending she didn't.

"I'm Alex Saavedra," he said, "and this is Dalton Wylie. We're detectives with the Berrendo Police Department."

She shifted her smile to the shorter blond man, then looked back at Saavedra and waited.

"The reason we're here," he explained, "is that there's been a problem at the high school and we thought you might be able to identify a suspect for us."

"I?" she asked.

"Show her the drawing," he said out of the side of his mouth.

She now noticed that Detective Wylie held a large sheet of manila paper rolled into a cylinder under his arm. Taking a few steps closer, he unrolled the paper, then held it for her to see the crudely sketched face of Buck Powell.

Saavedra asked, "Do you recognize him?"

She walked to the end of the sofa and turned on a lamp before looking again at the sketch. "It may bear a faint resemblance to a relative of my husband's."

"Who might that be, Mrs. Mulroney?"

"A second cousin or some such." She smiled as if bewildered. "The connection is distant."

"Do you know the cousin's name?"

She pretended to think, then shook her head. "If I ever did, I can't seem to remember."

Saavedra nodded as if her answer had been expected. "Is your son available?"

"His grandmother kept him home ill today." She laughed as if at an absurdity. "He's not playing hooky, if that's what you thought."

The detective smiled. "No, ma'am. Is he here, or with his grandparents?"

"He came home a little bit ago but went straight to bed."

He studied her for such a long moment, she felt certain he knew she was hiding something. But all he said was, "Do you think we could see him for a few minutes?"

She wondered what she would say if she had no notion why they had come. Making her decision, she asked, "What's this about, Detective?"

"The man in that drawing," he nodded at the paper the other detective had rolled back into a cylinder, "kidnapped a boy from the high school this morning. I believe you were there when we arrived on the scene."

"Kidnapped?" she whispered, hoping she sounded sufficiently shocked.

He nodded.

"That's terrible, but what does it have to do with Zeb?"

"That's what we're here to find out."

She held his gaze a moment longer, then moved to the phone and called Lupe in the kitchen. Keenly aware of the detectives listening, she said softly, "Lupe, go upstairs and see if Zeb is asleep. If he isn't, will you ask him to join us, please?"

"*Si, señora,*" the maid answered.

Thinking she was playing her hand adroitly, Alicia offered the detectives coffee, which they declined. When she invited them to sit down, they chose the wing chairs at both ends of the sofa. She sat in the middle and saw a light in the upstairs hall come on, illuminating the stairwell. A moment later, Zeb descended, wearing a black satin robe over gray pajamas and black leather slippers. Amused to see he had even mussed his hair to add to the illusion that he had just risen from bed, she gave him a small smile of congratulation as he entered the

131

room. He acknowledged her smile with a wan one, then folded himself in the closest chair and eyed the detectives with apparent annoyance as she introduced them.

Saavedra began with an apology. "I'm sorry to bother you, Zeb. I understand you stayed home sick today."

He didn't answer, merely waited with evident impatience.

"Show him the drawing," Saavedra told Wylie.

Wylie stood up and let the paper unfurl almost directly in front of Zeb's face.

Seeing the crude depiction of his cousin, Zeb couldn't resist a smile. "So?" he asked with a smirk.

"Recognize him?" Saavedra asked.

"It looks like a very poor portrait of my cousin."

"What's his name?"

"Buck Powell."

"Is that his real name?"

Zeb shrugged, then looked at his mother. "Does he have another name?"

"Not that I ever heard," she said, finishing with a tiny tinkle of laughter that made Zeb smile again.

Saavedra nodded for Wylie to put the drawing away. He rolled it against his left thigh, which he lifted slightly to provide a more horizontal surface. Thinking the detective on one foot looked ridiculous, Zeb shared a deeper smile with his mother. Saavedra thought they were a pair of cold sharks in a pool. Striving to keep his voice neutral, he asked, "When was the last time you saw your cousin, Zeb?"

He pretended to think. "Not for over a year." He again looked at his mother. "Isn't he in Denver?"

"That's right," she agreed. "He went up there seeking employment, didn't he?"

Zeb nodded, giving the detective a smugly blank look.

Saavedra knew they were lying, but he also knew he

couldn't press them the way he might someone else. Softly he asked Li'l Zeb, "Do you know Nathan Wheeler?"

"I've seen him around school."

"He's dating Amy Sterling. Didn't you use to go out with her?"

Zeb's smile was sinuous. "I date a lot of girls, Detective."

"Buck Powell kidnapped Nathan Wheeler from school today. Do you have any idea why he might do that?"

Zeb frowned. "Kidnapped him?"

Saavedra nodded.

"Why would anyone kidnap a poor boy?"

"More to the point," Saavedra said, "why would your cousin?"

"Buck's not real bright, but I didn't think he was that dumb."

"So you think he did it for money?"

"What other reason is there?"

"Revenge, jealousy, the desire to get even."

"Buck's been in Denver all last year. What could Nathan have done to him?"

"Maybe he did it to someone close to Buck. A cousin, for instance."

Zeb didn't flinch. "I can't quite place Nathan Wheeler. Do you have a picture of him, too?"

Saavedra shook his head. "Do you know where your cousin lives?"

"I think his parents have a trailer in Artesia. Is that right, Mother?"

"Maybe Atoka," she said.

"That sounds better," Zeb agreed. "Yes, I think they live in Atoka."

There was a momentary silence before she asked, "Is there anything else, gentlemen?"

Though he felt loath to leave with so little, Saavedra had to say, "No, I guess not."

Alicia stood up. "I'll call Lupe to show you out."

"We can find our way." He looked at the boy who obviously wasn't sick, at least not physically. "I'll probably have more questions later."

Zeb shrugged.

Alicia raised her eyebrows at the detectives, so they took their leave, Saavedra not concealing his disdain, Wylie hiding his by keeping his gaze on the floor. As soon as they were gone, she offered Zeb a drink on her way to the highboy.

"I'm having Dubonnet. Would you like some?"

"I'd rather have bourbon."

She laughed, reaching for the Jack Daniel's. "Your grandfather drinks bourbon." She poured two fingers in an old-fashioned glass. "Ice, spritzer?"

"Neat," he said.

After giving him the bourbon neat, she settled on the closest end of the sofa. "I think we did well, don't you?" She sipped her aperitif, then looked up to see he was staring at her with malevolence. "Don't look at me like that, Zeb. I'm on your side, remember?"

"Whose side were you on all those times Silas beat me?"

"I wanted so badly to help you, but what could I do?"

"You could've tried."

She set her glass down and walked to the window where she stood staring out at the brooding dark prairie and inky black groves. Finally she turned around and watched him sip his whiskey, looking so like a jaded rake the morning after that she had to smile. "You're such a handsome young man."

His eyes softened, meeting hers.

"Can you believe I didn't help because I was afraid?"

"He never hit you."

"That you know of."

"I've never seen any bruises."

She crossed the room slowly and deliberately, like a model on a runway. Closing the door quietly, she locked it, then returned to stand in front of him. She unbuttoned her skirt, stepped out of it and tossed it aside, turned her back and slid her slip up over her hips. When she pulled her pantyhose down, she heard the intake of his breath, and she smiled in satisfaction as she covered herself again, dropped her slip and retrieved her skirt. Buttoning it closed, she said, "He does it with a cigar."

Seeing his eyes burning bright, she sank to the floor in front of him. "So you see, I had good reason to be afraid."

His eyes were sullen now. "Someone should kill him."

"I suspect that's what you've done, using a surrogate."

He stared at her, unmoved.

"Is Nathan still alive?"

"He was when I left him."

"Good," she murmured, as if rewarding a performance. "Will he be able to identify you?"

He shook his head.

"Good," she said again, then smiled. "Let's make a pact, you and I, to protect each other from this moment on."

A cynical smile curled his lips. "It's a little late, don't you think?"

She shook her head. "It's only beginning."

When Silas came home, he found the door locked against him. He had known from the Lincoln Navigator in the driveway that his father was there, but he hadn't expected to be left out of the discussion of whatever had instigated the visit. When he knocked on the living room door, Old Zeb barked a command for whoever it was to let them be.

Silas went to his den, a room off-limits to everyone else but the maid. After selecting a cigar from the humidor, he stood at the window and looked out at the ghostly-lit rose garden as he drew the smoke deep into his lungs, unable to understand why his family hated him. Though he occasionally hurt them, in his son's case it was well-deserved punishment, and in his wife's, he considered it her duty to share his pain. Alicia, after all, had married into more wealth than her hillbilly clan could have hoped. Besides, the damage he inflicted was no more than he had endured at the hands of his father, the infamous old fart who at this very moment was keeping him locked out of the living room of his own home.

Knowing about anyone else what he knew about Old Zeb, Silas would expect the man to be sour. But Old Zeb's pleasures were vigorously robust. A gregarious regent of the country club, he was generous with local charities and a sugar daddy to a string of mistresses. Only to his son was he bitterly cruel, and Silas had never been able to fathom why. It hadn't been the disobedience of his marriage. The antipathy between them began long before that. On the one occasion he had garnered the courage to ask his mother, she said only that he was a willful child whose punishment was warranted. But he had tried hard to please his father.

Finishing his cigar, he again felt the cold indifference of his normal state of mind. As he started upstairs to change for dinner, he passed the now open door of the living room and allowed himself a casual glance inside.

Alicia and Li'l Zeb were alone. She was sitting on the floor in front of him while staring into her apparently empty glass. Wearing pajamas and a bathrobe, clothes Silas hadn't seen on him in years, Zeb leaned from his chair to tuck a strand of hair behind his mother's ear. The gesture gave Silas pause, so reminiscent was it of lovers.

Alicia met his eyes with a supercilious smile. "Your father wants you out at his house first thing tomorrow."

Silas thought the old man could have talked to him now rather than make him drive all the way to the valley in the morning, but he only shuddered as he continued climbing the stairs.

Chapter Eleven

"Who's that in your truck yonder?" Eldon Powell asked, lifting a curtain away from his living room window to look out at his floodlit yard.

"The boy's girlfriend," Devon answered, "and her mother."

Eldon sat down, peering at him from beneath the ridge of Neanderthal eye sockets. "They kin to you?"

He shook his head. "Mrs. Sterling is my landlady."

"Pretty tight, ain't you, to be riding around, the three of you, all cozy in your truck there, looking for the missing boy?"

"They asked for my help."

Eldon nodded. "My son's been in Denver nigh on a year. Ain't that right, Ma?"

"He left just 'fore Thanksgiving." She stood in the kitchen, leaning against the counter with her arms folded across her flaccid breasts. Meatloaf baking in the oven filled the trailer with the smell of tomatoes and onions sizzling in the grease of a cheap grade of beef.

"When did he get back?" Devon asked.

"He was parked in that self-same chair you're sitting in when I come home from work today. Was the first I'd seen him. How 'bout you, Ma?"

"Same for me. He come in the middle of Oprah."

"Did you know he was coming?"

Eldon shook his head. "We ain't friendly, me and Buck. We don't see what you call eye-to-eye on a lotta stuff."

Devon nodded.

"I didn't raise my son to be no thief," he said, "but that's what he is. Wasn't no doing of mine. I've been a working man all my life."

"Did you happen to notice the vehicle he was driving?"

"An old green Pontiac station wagon, all rusted out with Colorado plates, the tires half bald and a bad whine in the engine. Said it b'longed to a friend, but I hope his friend didn't pay much for it 'cause it sure as hell ain't worth nothing."

"Where's he staying?"

Eldon shook his head, then looked at his wife.

"He just got back," she said. "I guess he was figuring on staying with us like he done 'fore he left."

"I don't want him here," Eldon said. "Not if he's mixed up with this 'fore he's had time to stomp the dust of Denver off his shoes. If he's gonna start back in doing crime, he can stay somewhere else."

"Maybe he's with his cousin," Mrs. Powell said. "He picked him up at the airport in Albuquerque on Wednesday."

Eldon twisted all the way around to stare at her. "How'd Li'l Zeb know he was coming?"

"I called his mother," she said defensively.

"I told you I don't want to be asking them for no favors!"

"What'd it hurt? Li'l Zeb's got himself a fancy new sports car and prob'ly enjoyed the ride. I don't see no harm in letting a friendship grow 'tween the boys. Can't nothing be hurt by that."

Eldon looked disgusted as he turned back to Devon. " 'Cept my dumb son gets to do the rich kid's dirty work. Ain't that how you see it, Mr. Gray?"

"Could be what happened."

"Son of a bitch Mulroneys! They been screwing my family for three generations now. I've half a mind to take a thirty-ought over there and blow Ol' Zeb to hell!"

"Ol' Zeb ain't got nothing to do with this!" Mrs. Powell cried, as if she expected her husband to make good his threat.

"His li'l pipsqueak grandson does! Maybe I oughta shoot *him!*"

"You jus' leave the Mulroneys be!"

"That's what I told you to do! If you don't, why should I?"

"All I asked was a favor, one boy to another. I didn't go over there toting no shotgun!"

Eldon glowered at Devon. "You got any more good news to share?"

Devon gave him a commiserating smile. "You wouldn't know where Buck is now?"

Eldon shook his head. Devon looked at Mrs. Powell, who leaned back against the counter with a deflating sigh.

"What's gonna happen to him?" she asked. "Will he go back to prison?"

"If he's convicted."

"For how long?"

"That depends on what they did to Nathan Wheeler."

"My son had no reason to hurt that boy," she pleaded.

Devon and Eldon looked at each other, acknowledging reason wasn't apt to play a part in Nathan's fate. Devon stood up. "Thanks for talking to me."

"Don't come back," Eldon muttered.

Devon looked at Mrs. Powell, her face pinched with disappointment, then left them alone with the bad news he'd brought.

He could feel Lucinda and Amy watching from inside his truck as he walked across the floodlit yard. He got in and started the engine without saying anything, though the pressure of them waiting felt like water pushing against a dam. He drove to the northern outskirts of Artesia and stopped in the park along Eagle Draw, a concrete culvert that cradled one of the few perennial creeks still carrying runoff from the mountains. As he watched a breeze stir the golden leaves in a cottonwood beneath a streetlamp, he felt grateful that the women were letting him take his time to decide what he wanted to say.

He turned his back to the door so he could watch both their faces, but he looked at Amy when he said, "On Wednesday, Zeb picked up Buck at the airport in Albuquerque. They must've made their plan on the drive to Berrendo."

"So it *was* because of me," she whispered.

"I don't know their motive, but Buck spent the last year in Denver, so it's hard to figure he'd have anything to gain except pleasing Zeb."

Amy burst into tears, sobbing against her mother's breasts as Lucinda rocked her with silent comfort. Devon got out and walked a short distance away. He looked at the ridge of mountains, black silhouettes against the last stain of sunset, then toward the bluff above the Pecos River a few miles east, invisible in the creeping dark of night. Somewhere, not too distant from where he stood, Zeb and Buck held Nathan Wheeler at their mercy. Though he had no idea where to look, Devon felt impatient with the consummately useless activity of listening to Amy cry.

He drove south through Artesia, following a hunch that Buck's next order of business would be to get rid of the Pontiac as far from home as possible. That might mean El Paso or even Juárez, but it could be as close as Carlsbad, which put it within the realm of probability that he could find it.

Amy blew her nose, then sniffled a while before the three of them rode in a silence broken only by the drone of the engine and hum of the tires. Seeing a tavern ahead, he glanced with casual curiosity at the cars in the lot. On the very edge of light he saw an old green station wagon. He pulled to the side of the road, made a u-turn and drove back, shut off his engine and studied the car. It didn't have Colorado plates, but in all other particulars matched the description.

"Keep the doors locked," he told Lucinda, noting Amy seemed okay now. "If anyone bothers you, lay on the horn."

Lucinda nodded.

"Amy," he said, "I want you to watch the door. If Buck comes out, don't say anything. He's got no reason to connect me to what's going on, so we'll follow him on the chance he'll lead us to Nathan."

She nodded, her eyes bright with a hope that tore at his heart as he walked across the desert gravel to the tavern's front door.

"You know what happens after someone dies?" the man asked as Milt set a fresh beer in front of him.

Tall with a bony face and a sweeping black moustache, Milt Hooper was the owner of The Bat's Cave as well as its bartender, bouncer, janitor and handyman. Riding the rail of fifty, he had been divorced twice and was sending child support to a third woman who claimed to have his kid. Milt never took the issue to court, he simply paid the woman to stay out of his life, which was what he generally wanted of his customers. He could be amiable as long as they returned the favor while spending their money. Anything beyond that was a breach of the unwritten contract he figured everyone agreed to when they entered his tavern. In his experience, discussions of the afterlife tended not to be amiable, so he was about to move away when the burly blond said, "You get buffeted by the winds of karma."

That stopped Milt because his new girlfriend was always talking about karma and reincarnation, stuff he initially had thought sounded crazy but was coming around to think maybe made sense. He gave the guy an encouraging look in the hope he would learn something new to throw at Madge the next time she started talking about previous lives.

"It's s'posed to be godawful," Buck said, using his thumb to wipe the beer froth off his upper lip.

"How do you know?" Milt scoffed. "Were you there?"

"We've all been there thousands of times. No kidding. I read this book when I was in lock-up." He grinned. "One thing about jail is you got a lotta time to read."

Milt congratulated himself for having pinned the guy as an ex-con. There was an edge to men who had served time that a bartender learned to recognize after a while.

"I read this one book," Buck went on, "about being dead in Tibet. It said after you die it's like you fall into this weightless state, like the astronauts, you know? And while you're floating around, there's all these howling winds blowing you every which way." He waved his hands in the air. "They sound like an avalanche and a flash flood and a hurricane and a tornado all at the same time, and what it is, see, is all the bad things you did when you were alive. Every little thing you think nobody noticed—the big ones, too, a'course—they all gang up and come down on you hard and it hurts like hell," he paused to chuckle, " 'cause that's what it is, that's what the Christians call it. All this pain blows you this way and that, and while you're tumbling howling through this dark nightmare, you see a man and a woman fucking, and 'cause you got the same negative stuff in your karma they got in theirs, you get sucked into 'em like you're being pulled down a drain and—bam!—you're a baby waiting to be born."

Milt stared a moment, then said, "That's the most depressing thing I ever heard. You go around believing that and you're apt to put a bullet in your brain."

Buck laughed. "Think of the karmic wind that'd cause!"

Milt wiped the counter, remembering a friend he had lost to suicide. "You think it's worse'n killing someone else?"

"Depends. If you do it to stop yourself from killing someone else, then it'd be a good thing."

He nodded. "I can see that."

"According to this book, your intentions count as much as what you do. So if you kill someone by accident, it ain't as bad as deliberately setting out to do what the law calls premeditated murder. It's more like manslaughter."

"I never could figure," Milt said, "why slaughter was less serious than murder."

" 'Cause it's what we do to animals. According to this book, you're accountable for every fish you catch, deer you shoot or cow you eat a steak outta. Killing anything's bad karma, but killing people is the worst, and that's why there's a special word for it."

Milt studied the pale eyes in front of him. "You've given this some thought."

Buck shrugged. "When you're not reading in jail, you're mostly thinking."

Milt nodded. "So how does a person get to be good?"

"I figure it takes a miracle."

He laughed. "What'd the book say?"

"That you're s'posed to meditate a lot and make yourself useful. It said the best prayer is, 'Bless me with usefulness.' "

Milt fumbled in his pocket for his cigarettes, suddenly clumsy in doing something he did forty times a day without trying. He got the cigarette in his mouth and lit it, then looked at his customer through the veil of smoke.

"Sometimes though," Buck said, "when I try to be useful is when I fuck up the worst."

Milt looked down to exhale a jet of smoke that hit the floor and bounced back in a cloud around his knees. "How's that?"

Buck sipped his beer. "When you're trying to help somebody, whether you do good or not depends on what they're doing, don't it?"

"But if it's your intention that counts, then the results don't matter."

"Even if someone gets hurt real bad?"

Milt sucked on his cigarette, wondering what Buck had done. "You're the one read the book. What's it say?"

"It didn't deal with that situation." The energy that had driven him earlier was depleted, so he looked like a tire going flat. He was sitting directly across from the door, and just then someone came in, silhouetting Buck's bulk against the neon outside.

Milt waited for the newcomer to straddle a stool at the other end of the bar before he approached. As easily as he had pinned Buck as an ex-con, he recognized this customer as an off-duty cop, or maybe undercover. There was an affinity between the way cops and criminals watched the world, which Milt figured wasn't surprising since they were on opposite sides of the same game.

Hearing the newcomer order a draft, Buck felt as if a blade were being drawn down his spine with just enough force to cut his shirt but not break his skin. He didn't have to, but he looked anyway, recognizing the vacationing cop he had sat next to in Denny's that morning.

"Sonofabitch," he whispered to himself, though staring at the cop as he was, the message was relayed between them. The fucker smiled. Buck took a five from his wallet, tossed it on the bar and left without waiting for change.

Outside in the harsh glare of neon, he saw the faces of a

woman and a girl watching him from inside a Dodge pickup. The girl seemed familiar, and Buck thought maybe he had seen her at the high school when he went back the second time. It was an eerie coincidence to see both the cop and a girl from Berrendo so far south.

The door opened behind him. He turned around to see the cop less than two feet away. Feeling trapped, he told himself the woman and girl weren't defensive ends in this game. It was between him and the cop, who was smiling as if to apologize for almost running into him in the doorway. Buck walked over to the cruddy Pontiac he hated. Having left it unlocked, he got in without delay, cranked the engine and tried to appear calm as he spun onto the highway.

He was breathing hard when he looked in his mirror and saw the pickup a hundred yards behind. That the cop would take a woman and girl on a tail didn't seem right, but he couldn't think of any other explanation for why they were there.

In Carlsbad, he stopped at Denny's for supper. He hadn't seen the Dodge for the last twenty minutes, so figured he must have lost the cop, though not because of anything he'd done. Maybe the pickup had a flat or some kind of breakdown. All he knew was the Dodge was gone and he was hungry.

He took the last seat at the counter, way down close to the bathrooms. It was full dark outside and he felt like a target with his back to the window, but the restaurant was crowded with Friday night business and he didn't guess there was much likelihood of anyone shooting him.

The waitress was puny with a pimply face. He watched her pencil move on her order pad as he ordered a burger combo and Coke. When she brought his drink, he busied himself unwrapping his straw. Behind him a family was making noise.

He turned around to see what the fuss was about and saw a grandma and fat momma with five brats squabbling over the crayons the waitress had given them. Each kid only had one and they all wanted a color they didn't have. The grandma and momma were talking between themselves, ignoring the kids.

Buck looked along the line of loners at the counter, single men like himself, most of them a little lower down on their luck than he was. In several booths he noticed teenagers wearing the red-on-black howling coyote. It made him wonder if he was being plagued by guilt or if kids these days used the highway between Berrendo and Carlsbad as one giant strip for cruising. When the waitress brought his food, he garnered the courage to look at her pimply face and ask, "How come there're so many kids from Berrendo here tonight?"

She smiled, making him think she might be pretty when her zits cleared up. "There's a football game 'tween the high schools. It's always been a big deal, the rivalry 'tween the Coyotes and Cavemen."

Buck laughed so loud she blushed. As he watched her hurry away—the restaurant was packed, every table full—he thought such an ugly woman couldn't have a boyfriend. Maybe he'd stick around and take her home when she got off. She'd probably be grateful for a little attention, and morning would be soon enough for the drive to El Paso. No need to worry now that he knew the cop had come south for football.

Food was delivered to the noisy table behind him, so the kids quieted down. He was just starting to feel comfy when he looked over his shoulder and saw the cop come in the front door behind the woman and girl. Buck reminded himself they were here for the game. Maybe they were even a family. Just because the cop had eaten breakfast at Denny's didn't necessarily mean he was single. Waiting for the hostess, the cop let his gaze wander down the men at the counter until he saw Buck. Their eyes locked, as they had when Buck was waiting for the light while the cop watched him from inside the Denny's in Berrendo. Then as now, he felt caught by the cop's eyes.

There was no empty table, so the cop and his women sat down to wait. Buck bolted his hamburger and folded the fries into his mouth without bothering with ketchup. He kept telling himself they were here to watch football, arguing the cop wouldn't bring a woman and a girl, for Christ's sake, on a tail. Maybe the cop had simply pinned him for an ex-con and hated anyone who'd ever served time. Their seeing each other again was just a coincidence that was making him sick when he didn't need to pay it any mind.

He sucked air through his straw, wishing he had more Coke. But he didn't have much money. If he didn't sell the car soon, he'd be spending the night in the cold like that kid in the cooler. Bound and gagged on a metal floor with only a dripping pipe for company.

He looked at the cop leaning close to the woman as she whispered something in his ear. The girl was watching them. A pretty girl, well filled out. The woman wasn't bad either. Maybe she was a widow and the cop was doing them both. Just then he looked up. Buck figured his own smile must have been sleazy because the one the cop gave back was scolding, as if the fucker could read his mind.

God, how he hated cops. He wished he could drive his fist deep into this one's gut and make him puke in front of his lady friend. Or maybe she was his wife. Most cops were married. A lot of felons were, too. Zeb intended to marry that girl whose downfall had caused all this trouble. Buck thought she must be some piece if Li'l Zeb was willing to take her as is. Behind him, he heard the woman say, "Hurry back, Amy."

He jerked around to see the girl walk past on her way to the can. He stared too long, watching her butt beneath the black sweatshirt riding her hips, then he gave the cop another smile. This time he didn't smile back.

Buck stood up, grabbed his check and stalked down the aisle between the counter and row of booths by the windows, heading straight toward the cop because the bench for waiting was across from the cash register.

With his back to the cop, he stood in line to pay. When his turn came, the cashier messed up his change. He had to argue with her about it, the cop all the time listening, so he felt the maw of a trap at his neck. When he had his money clutched in his hand, the right amount of change he'd had to fight for, he turned around to face the cop. A message flashed between them like a stab of lightning, a mutual recognition that, because of the girl, the stakes of their game were now deadly.

Chapter Twelve

Devon followed Buck outside, then stood in the shadow of a cypress and watched the Pontiac pull into traffic heading north. He was turning the ignition in his pickup when Amy pounded on the window of the passenger side. Behind her, Lucinda's face flashed ghostly pale in the pan of headlights from a passing car. Devon leaned over and opened the door.

"Were you going to leave us behind?" Amy asked as she slid across the seat, followed by her mother.

He was backing out of the space before Lucinda closed the door. "Evidently not," he muttered.

Amy shut up after that, and he held his awareness of having hurt her in abeyance as he searched the traffic ahead for a glimpse of the Pontiac. He saw it cruise through an intersection on a yellow light. Swerving into a gas station, he circled the pumps and came out headed west on the cross street, then made a right on 285 again.

"Pretty cool," Amy offered in peace.

"If not strictly legal," Lucinda teased.

Both of them wore smiles soliciting recognition. "I shouldn't have brought you," he said.

Their smiles disappeared, Lucinda's beneath somber eyes weighing the severity of his regret. But Amy retorted, "Why would you be here without us? I mean, who's Buck Powell to you?"

"Amy," Lucinda cautioned softly.

"She's right," he conceded. "I'm not a cop on assignment. Guess I forgot that for a minute."

"Or two," Amy said.

He laughed. "Maybe even five or ten."

"You miss it, don't you," Lucinda murmured.

Thinking that in his years on the force he had never tailed a man anywhere near the distance he was traveling tonight, mostly because his jurisdiction had been confined to the city limits, he toyed with the idea of going to Austin and applying to the Texas Rangers so he would have room to maneuver, then remembered there was more than one complication to stop him from doing that. When he finally answered Lucinda's question with a silent nod, his reticence kept the women quiet through the dark stretch of road between towns.

Under the lights of Artesia, they watched the station wagon turn west on Highway 82 toward the mountains. He glanced at his gauge, then pulled into the Exxon station on the corner.

"Can I run to Burger King and get us some supper?" Amy asked eagerly.

"If you're not back by the time my tank's full," he warned, "I'll leave you behind."

Taking the wallet her mother offered, Amy tumbled from the truck as he got out the other side. Lucinda walked around and looked across the hood to watch her running toward the restaurant. The backs of her sneakers were striped with reflective chevrons that flashed as her heels rose and fell beneath the flag of her long black hair above her sleek little butt.

Devon slid his hands into his pockets and listened to the chime of the pump as he stared into the dark where Buck's taillights had disappeared.

Lucinda asked softly, "Would you really leave her behind?"

He smiled, hoping to make her feel welcome again. "Not without you."

"We'd be stranded without a car and, as far as you know, no money either."

"I'm pretty sure you have a credit card. There's a motel right down the block."

She glanced at The Thunderbird Lodge with its prominent vacancy sign. "Would you come back for us?"

"Only if you had your own room."

She laughed. "That would be fun."

He nodded. "Under different circumstances."

She sighed, looking over the hood of his truck to where Amy stood at the counter inside Burger King. "Do you think Nathan's still alive?"

The pump chimed as he took his time answering. Finally he said, "There's always that chance."

She met his eyes. "Thanks for bringing us. Amy would go crazy just sitting home waiting to hear."

The pump quit and it was suddenly quiet. She came close and wrapped her arms around his waist under his jacket, her cheek against his shirt. He let her rest a moment, then unwound her arms and leaned down for a quick kiss that ended the moment without lessening its intimacy. She smiled. "Do you realize how much of a sweetheart you are?"

He took the nozzle out of his tank and rehung it on the pump. "I'll go pay for the gas."

Chief of Police Arthur Hudson frowned at the two detectives sitting in front of his desk. "How'd he get there before you did?"

Saavedra shrugged. "As near as we can tell, he's got Mrs. Sterling and her daughter with him. Maybe Amy knew where to find Buck's parents."

"You didn't think to ask?"

"I told her mother to take her home," Saavedra bristled. "I expected to find 'em there, but when I went by, nobody answered the bell. A neighbor told me the three of 'em took off in his pickup about an hour after they left here."

"So we not only got a dangerous suspect on the loose, we've got three civilians on his tail, apparently a helluva lot closer'n we are!"

"We don't know that."

"What *do* you know?"

"The Mulroney boy's in it up to his eyeballs, but I couldn't get anything close to an admission out of him."

"You stay away from the Mulroneys. If it turns out Li'l Zeb *is* involved, there won't be room for mistakes when we try'n prove it."

He swiveled his chair around to look out the window of his second-story office. A block east, Main Street was a bright ribbon of cruising teenagers mingled with truckers because 285 was the only north-south corridor in this part of the state. A block north, 2nd Street, a.k.a. Highway 380, served the same purpose east-west. The rest of town consisted of residential neighborhoods with one street lamp and a few lit porches on each block. Otherwise only the blue lights of televisions muted through windows added to the illumination.

He wondered how many people watching those televisions knew about the kidnapping. The local broadcast station was a student program from the university in Portales, ninety miles northeast. Rather than reporters roaming at large, they gleaned their stories from official sources, which so far he'd kept quiet. The *Daily Register* had no Saturday edition, so the story wouldn't hit print until Sunday, but word of mouth could spread news as fast as media. Every family with a child at Berrendo High had certainly heard about the vice principal delivering Nathan Wheeler to an imposter posing as a cop. Children were being hugged a little closer this Friday night, school officials on the phone dealing with more than the usual complaints from a community normally divided on such comparatively benign issues as evolution versus creationism, and church services were being attended rather than the football game, which had been canceled because the district superintendent didn't want the parents congregating until Nathan was home.

Hudson told the detectives behind him, "The sheriff's posse'll be mounted at dawn. We've set up roadblocks, and every officer we've got is on the street checking anyone who farts." He turned around and looked at his two best. "You're supposed to be the diplomats. The mouth of our department. I don't want you shaking up the Mulroneys unnecessarily, but if it's at all possible under God's blue sky, I want Nathan Wheeler found alive."

"We all want that," Wylie mumbled.

Hudson nodded. "I just spoke to the vice principal's wife. She said Tom's bawling in the bathroom. I'm not telling you that for public dissemination, but I want you to know no one regrets what happened more'n him."

"Except Nathan Wheeler," Saavedra said.

"Yeah, 'cept him." He looked down at the papers blanketing his desk, blind to their importance. In desperation he looked back at his top detectives. "Ain't you got any more leads?"

Saavedra shrugged. "We put out an APB on the Pontiac. Buck left his parents two hours before we got there, so he could be anywhere. Between when he arrived at their trailer and when he left school is a five-hour gap, which leaves us with a bigger anywhere. Except for knowing we have to search a two-hundred-mile radius, all we got is a strong suspicion Zeb Mulroney's pulling the strings. But since we gotta handle him with kid gloves . . ." He finished with a shrug.

Hudson caught himself wishing he hadn't quit smoking. "Who else was there when you questioned Li'l Zeb?"

"His mother."

"Prob'ly bring a lawyer if we pull him in."

The detectives watched him with noncommittal faces.

"Ol' Zeb's had Ambrose Scott on retainer for thirty years. He's hell on contracts but ain't touched a criminal case that I can remember."

Saavedra licked his lips.

"All right," Hudson said.

They were heading for the door when he stopped them.

"Try'n bring Silas with him. There's bad blood 'tween 'em like I've never seen 'tween father and son," he paused, remembering, "unless it's Ol' Zeb and Silas." He studied his detectives. "We'll try'n keep the old man in the dark long as we can."

He heaved himself from his chair and followed them out, but turned the opposite direction, slowly making his way toward the canteen. It was empty, all his men on the street looking for a kid who must be scared shitless, if he was still alive. Hudson swung the cigarette machine around so he could get at it from behind. He took out a pack, tore it open and lit up with matches someone had left on a table, telling himself if this wasn't Marlboro Country the damn place didn't exist.

"We're going the wrong way," Amy said.

The prairie around them was dark, not even a moon to keep the headlights company on the blacktop road. She still held a cup of leftover ice she occasionally rattled. Their hamburgers and fries had been eaten, the wrappings crumpled in a bag at Lucinda's feet. The coffee cups were also trash in the bag. Without more coffee, they were as useless as the road stretching in front of the truck was apparently empty.

"This is the way he was heading," Devon said.

"But Nathan's behind us," she argued. "I can feel him pulling me back."

He looked in the rearview mirror, watching the world disappear as soon as his tires left it behind. "There's a lot of country back there." He kept the speedometer nudging sixty, not daring to go faster because a high-speed collision with deer or antelope could kill them all. As beat-up as the Pontiac was, Buck couldn't do much better even if he wasn't worried about colliding with wildlife, so Devon figured he had a good chance to catch up as long as they were still on the same road.

"Please turn around," Amy whimpered.

He glanced at Lucinda, not wanting his eyes off the road longer than that, but she was looking at Amy, puzzled over her daughter's sudden declaration of telepathy. Without breaking speed, he asked, "You got any idea where to look back there?"

"No," she answered, her voice shaky.

"The man in front of us knows exactly where Nathan is. I think we're better off following him."

"But where is he? We haven't seen him for hours!"

"Thirty minutes."

"He could've taken any of these dirt roads we've passed. Maybe he turned around and that's why I'm feeling pulled back!"

"What if we make it all the way to Artesia without seeing him? Then what?"

Amy kept quiet.

"Would you want to go home?"

"No," she said.

"We wouldn't have much choice, 'cause if he did turn around he could be anywhere by now."

"Maybe I'll feel where to go."

Never having worked with a psychic detective, it took him a minute to come up with an answer. "If we haven't spotted him by the time we reach Mayhill, we'll go back."

"There's not even a motel in Mayhill. Why would he stop?"

"Is there a tavern?"

"Every town's got a tavern."

Lucinda gave him a smile, so he figured she agreed with his decision not to follow Amy's instinct to nowhere. Not that he thought she was wrong—Nathan probably was behind them—but back there included a good stretch of the Pecos Valley. He figured there must be a thousand adobe huts, abandoned barns and boarded-up businesses, not to mention the numerous arroyos that could serve as adequate hiding places for a body.

"I bet Nathan's hungry." Amy looked at Devon with pleading eyes. "Do you think they fed him?"

"I don't know."

Her voice trembled when she asked, "Or even gave him a drink of water?"

"Honey," Lucinda crooned, pulling her close.

"Don't think about it," he said. "It'll make you crazy."

"How can I not think about him?" she whispered.

"Think about how you can help him. Keep your mind sharp so you'll be ready if you get that chance."

She sat up straight and shook the ice in her cup, bent her head to the straw and sucked water from the bottom. Then she said, "You're smart, Devon. I bet you were a good cop."

"Thanks," he said.

"Why'd you quit?"

The road stretched long and lonely in front of them, Mayhill still forty miles away. He decided this was as good a time as any to tell them why he surrendered his badge in what should have been the prime of his career.

"I was working a case where a prostitute was accused of killing her husband," he said, winding into it slow. "They were alone when the cops arrived, and her prints were the only ones on the weapon, but she claimed someone else did it. Their apartment was on the ground floor on an alley. She said a man they both knew had been visiting, and while she was in the kitchen making supper, he picked the gun up off the coffee table, shot her husband, put the gun back and went out through the window. When she heard the shot, she ran into the living room in time to see the man leave."

He remembered the layout of the apartment, the husband's blood on the carpet, the half-cooked goulash still on the stove.

"I should have taken myself off the case 'cause Alma—that was her name—she and I were friends." He looked across Amy's intensely-listening face to meet Lucinda's eyes, but all he could see was her reflection in the window as she stared out at the dark they were traveling through.

Amy grimaced, acknowledging the delicacy of his admission. "Why didn't you?"

Devon watched the road in front of him a moment before saying, "The evidence against her was pretty strong, so another detective might not have tried hard enough to help her."

"But you did 'cause she was your friend."

"Yeah." He remembered taking her to cheap hotels where she would service him on her knees, or sometimes they'd do it in his city-issued sedan parked in a dark alley. She would throw his handkerchief out the window after doing the clean up, then he'd drive her back to whatever corner she was working that night. One time he had offered to buy her dinner, but she said her husband didn't want her going out with other men. "When you're not working," he'd teased. "Yeah," she'd said, her eyes so sad. After she was in jail, he'd ordered an AIDS test and told her the results himself, watching her pick at a hangnail until he caught hold of her hands to stop her from making it worse.

"So what happened?" Amy asked.

He tried to shuffle the deck to the shortest run of cards that would tell enough of the story. "Her husband had been dealing drugs, so at first I thought that was the link between him and the killer, but it turned out they were both actors in the worst kind of porno films." Again he glanced at Lucinda. This time she was staring at him with a silent plea that he not educate Amy on what happened in those films.

"Yech," Amy said.

"Yeah, they were bad," he agreed. "When I tried to trace the actor through the studio, I learned their business was being shielded by another detective on the force."

"You mean a policeman was protecting them?"

He nodded. "I'd gone to him for help and confided the whole scenario, not knowing he was tipping off the suspect I was trying to nab."

Off to the left he saw eyes catching red from his headlights. From their height, he guessed he was seeing deer, and he willed them to stay put until the prairie was again a black void on both sides of the road.

"So what did you do?" Amy asked.

Once the words were out there was no taking them back. By saying them, he chanced prosecution and prison, but the two women watching him seemed more important, their gift of wanting him in their lives.

"I tried to convince him to help me shut down the operation, put the killers on death row and let Alma die in the dignity of freedom rather than jail, but he kept trying to pull me in, offering money as if that could compensate for all the damage they were doing. Finally I pretended to go along and walked him out to his car. All the way there, he kept saying how I wouldn't regret the decision I'd made. As he was unlocking his door, I told him I hoped he was right."

He stopped again, his mind sorting through other paths out of the box he'd put himself in for the sake of being honest with two women who considered him worthy of admiration. They waited in silence, their attention focused so intensely he didn't need to look to know they were watching him. But he did look, at Amy first, her young face as yet unmarred by the tragedy she was on the brink of enduring, then he met Lucinda's eyes and said, "As he was getting into his car, I pulled his gun from the back of his belt, put the barrel behind his ear and pulled the trigger."

Lucinda's eyes said she had expected that end to his story, had seen it coming, and felt betrayed now with her daughter between them.

Amy's face was blank, her eyes shiny with shock. "Did he die?" she whispered.

"On the spot." He watched only the road for the minutes they traveled in silence.

"And they never found out it was you?"

He shook his head.

After a moment, she asked, "*Do* you regret it?"

"Part of me does."

"And part doesn't?"

"That's right."

"So you quit being a cop even though no one knew?"

He nodded.

"All that happened in El Paso just before you moved to Berrendo and rented our apartment?"

"Yeah."

She sighed. "Maybe it happened so you could be here to help us now."

"The two don't have anything to do with each other."

"Everything's connected. All of life's an endless river that never stops pulling everyone into the future."

She leaned against his shoulder, which surprised him, the immediacy of her mercy, but when he looked at the woman who had raised such a precious child, he saw her forgiveness wouldn't be so easy.

Chapter Thirteen

Alex Saavedra clipped his nails as he sat in a chair tilted against the wall of Chief Hudson's office. Beside him, Dalton Wylie pulled at a whisker he had missed shaving almost thirteen hours earlier. Behind his desk, Chief Hudson was chainsmoking cigarettes after three years on the wagon. Silas Mulroney, the suspect's father, stood by the door puffing on a cigar. The knowledge that the cigar cost more than Saavedra's shirt had something to do with the opinion he was trying to express by clipping his nails during the interrogation.

The boy known around town as Li'l Zeb was slumped insolently in a chair in front of the desk, his right ankle crossed on his left knee. The loafer thus extended was so new there was hardly any dirt on the sole. His sock was the same soft gray as his trousers, which were made from some material Saavedra's mother would say draped well, and his blue shirt had obviously been tailored to fit out of a smoky fabric Alex guessed might be silk. The pulse throbbing in the kid's throat was the only indication he was under stress.

"So you picked him up at the airport on Wednesday?" Saavedra asked.

Zeb nodded, his hazel eyes cold as clay.

Saavedra snipped the tip off his thumbnail. "This afternoon you said you hadn't seen Buck since before he left for Denver."

"Guess I forgot."

"Forgot you drove to Albuquerque the day before yesterday?"

"I was sick. Remember?"

"Oh yeah. Your grandma kept you home 'cause you had a tummy ache."

"She was nice enough to call in for me."

Saavedra watched the kid's pulse throb. "Did Buck say anything about planning to kidnap Nathan Wheeler?"

Zeb shook his head. "I had no idea they knew each other."

"They probably didn't."

"Then how do you explain what happened?" the kid asked in a falsely baffled tone.

"I think you were pissed 'cause Nathan took Amy away from you."

Li'l Zeb was mad. "I broke up with *her*."

"Why?"

"She wouldn't put out."

Saavedra looked at Silas, thinking the chief had been right about bad blood between them. Any other father would make an effort to protect his son, but Silas was enjoying watching him squirm. Not that Zeb was losing his cool. Not yet anyway.

Snip, snip, snip with the clippers, then Saavedra dropped them in his shirt pocket. "You're used to getting what you want, aren't you, Zeb?"

"It's generally been my experience."

"And when Amy wouldn't put out, that made you mad."

"There're plenty of girls who will."

"Was she putting out for Nathan?"

"She won't anymore."

The words hung in the air as Saavedra slowly smiled. "Why's that?"

For the first time the boy looked to his father for help. In response, Silas blew a smoke ring at the ceiling. Zeb glowered at both detectives with the bounty of his animosity, then zeroed in on the chief. "I want a lawyer."

"Your father waived that privilege," Saavedra said, "and being as you're a minor, what he says is what counts."

Zeb shifted his malevolence back to the interrogating detective. "Not anywhere outside this room."

Saavedra figured the kid was probably right. Also that his mother had called Old Zeb as soon as they left the house, which meant the kid's wish would be granted in not too many more minutes. Leaving the chances of a conviction for future consideration, he pushed for any clue to Nathan's whereabouts. "Does Buck have an apartment, a cabin in the mountains, a camper parked in an arroyo somewhere?"

Zeb smiled. "Buck's from Artesia, so he probably knows Lea County better than Chaves. That's a lot of territory to cover, isn't it, Detective?"

Saavedra nodded. "If Nathan's found alive, it'll go easier on both you and Buck."

Zeb shrugged. "Nothing I can do about that."

"You mean he's not alive now?"

"I mean I don't know anything about it, so you're wasting your time."

The chief's phone rang, one abrupt twang shattering the tension. Everyone knew it was over, the chance come and gone. The chief picked up, but before he could say anything, Ambrose Scott strode into the room. He wore casual clothes and was breathing hard, his face red with the exertion of his hurry. Hudson grunted into the phone, "He's already here," then hung up as he met the eyes of Old Zeb's attorney.

"I'm surprised at you, Art," Scott scolded. "You know

better'n this." He told Li'l Zeb in a more kindly tone, "Let's go, son. If they have any more questions, they'll have to charge you with a crime before they can ask 'em."

"We might just do that," Saavedra muttered.

Scott glanced at him, then faced Silas in the corner. "Did you waive your right to an attorney?"

"I'm an attorney," he answered.

Scott hissed, took hold of Li'l Zeb's arm and propelled him through the door. Silas followed sheepishly.

The three officers listened to the elevator close at the end of the hall; then Hudson looked at his detectives and said sadly, "He did it."

Saavedra nodded. "But we haven't got any more hint of where to look than we had before."

"Which was none," Wylie mumbled.

"No trace of Buck?"

Both detectives shook their heads.

"What about that cop from El Paso?"

"His truck's got Texas plates," Saavedra said, "and Austin hasn't responded to our request for registration, so all we know is he's driving a brown pickup. The neighbor didn't even know the make."

"What about the El Paso P.D.?"

Wylie snorted. "They told me to call again next week when a Lieutenant Dreyfus'll be back from vacation."

"Sonofabitch," Hudson said.

Saavedra nodded. "I'm having trouble believing he'd tail a suspect with the girl and her mother along, but it looks like that's what he's doing."

"Merciful God," Hudson moaned. "If we lose another kid. . . .

"We haven't lost Nathan yet," Saavedra argued, but it sounded weak even to him.

* * * * *

The village of Mayhill was nestled around a curve in the road. The town was comprised of a restaurant, general store, post office and realty, all housed in a two-story rock building that looked a hundred years old, but only the tavern across the street was open. Three vehicles were parked in front, none of them a station wagon. Drifting through town on the commodious curve, Devon saw the Pontiac half-hidden in brush beside a ramshackle cabin.

It hadn't occurred to him that Buck might have a friend in the mountains. But since the cabin was dark, it was equally likely he was sleeping in his car. Devon turned around at the entrance to James Canyon, then drove back, cut his engine and coasted into the shadow of a stand of ponderosa twenty yards from the station wagon and on the same side of the road. He sat in a silence broken only by the ticking of escaping heat as he studied the cabin for a reaction inside. Seeing none, he looked at the women.

Lucinda was watching him warily, her expression at best noncommittal. Not having spotted the Pontiac's hiding place, Amy was looking around. When she felt his attention, she met his eyes and waited.

"I'll be right back," he said, easing the door open. He left it ajar and crossed the road, empty as far as he could see, which wasn't a great distance because it curved in both directions.

The moon had finally risen above the trees, so the shadows were long, duplicating everything with black velvet silhouettes. A light wind shifting the shapes made the world seem unstable, while the scrabble of leaves bouncing down the road lent an eerie soundtrack to the scene. He skirted the fringe of the forest to approach the Pontiac, looking in from afar, then up close. The station wagon was empty, which could mean Buck was inside the cabin or had taken a blanket into the woods. He may even have left with someone else or in a vehicle stashed here for that purpose.

Devon eased up on the cabin. No drapes blocked his view of the front room, illuminated by the moon so he could see no one was there. Which said nothing about whether Buck's friend was home. He could be asleep in the back room, or maybe Buck had a key and an open invitation, or maybe it was his cabin. The front yard had been recently raked, but the back was cluttered with leaves, making a silent survey impossible. The curtains on those windows were closed anyway.

Devon returned to his truck and opened the door, causing the dome light to come on. "I'm going to the tavern," he whispered. "If you need me, blow the horn." He eased the door shut and walked away, feeling the women's eyes on his back.

Lucinda watched him walk along the edge of the road, not as hidden as before, and caught herself wishing he would make more effort to conceal himself from whoever might be watching inside the cabin. She glanced at the steering column, saw his keys in the ignition and felt reassured. But whether he had left them as a message that he deserved her trust in return or merely as a precaution in case she needed to snatch Amy out of danger, she didn't know.

When he crossed the road in the light from the tavern, she saw him almost as she had the first time he had come to her door: an inconspicuously handsome man, seemingly stalwart and steady, kindness being the predominant front he presented. Beneath that benign surface, however, she had sensed even then an undercurrent of danger. Some undefined contradiction behind his eyes, a suggestion of irony in his smiles, a hint that neither he nor the world were exactly on the level.

She had credited it to his being an ex-cop, someone savvy to wild city streets. In a small town, the appeal of a man familiar with the underbelly of a metropolis was undiluted by his subtle suggestion of being adept at violence.

But she had expected him to act only in defense and couldn't understand how what he had done helped anyone. Corruption was ubiquitous, cops on the take interchangeable, which probably meant the murdered detective had been replaced before Devon left town. She could see that as a tragedy in itself, but the sacrifice of his career wasn't her concern. It was the safety of her daughter in the company of a man she had allowed into their lives.

Yet in all the years following Lyle's death, no other man had elicited from her such a visceral response. She remembered the first time he touched her. She had been belatedly cleaning out the fireplace, scraping the little shovel's blade across the bricks to push the accumulated ashes down the chute. Apparently he had been walking by and heard the scraping, because by the time she went outside to collect the ashes, he had already transferred them to a cardboard box. Since he had used his hands to fill it, she naturally invited him into her kitchen to wash.

When she gave him a towel, their fingers brushed against each other, forcing her to retreat girlishly, her hands behind her back. He was surprised by her reaction, she saw that in his eyes. When she offered him coffee, he asked if that was really what she wanted in the middle of a lazy afternoon. She shook her head and took another step away, which meant her back was against the refrigerator, leaving no more room to retreat.

He kept his distance, his eyes and smile saying how much he liked her while he asked, "When's your daughter coming home?"

"Not till late," she had answered.

"Then we have time," he said, coming close enough to kiss her.

He didn't touch her with his hands, though he lingered in his kiss enough to caress her lips with his tongue, making her womb contract with longing. She didn't know how else to describe the yearning she felt. When he had withdrawn and was searching her face for any hint of response, she raised her hand and touched his cheek, feeling the prickle of whiskers. It had been so long since she had been intimate with anyone, her yearning overpowered her caution as she pressed herself close and kissed him again.

They almost did it there in the kitchen. At the last moment she came to her senses and invited him into her bedroom. He had laughed and said that was probably a good idea, and she felt so pleased leading him down the hall to her room. Naked on the sheet, the covers thrown heedlessly to the floor, she felt their first coupling was like coming home, though she didn't tell him that, afraid he would think she was staking a claim.

Had it been just this morning that she prodded him to make their relationship public? He obliged her by offering to take them to the game in Carlsbad, and after that invited her to spend a weekend in the mountains. As it turned out, they did go to Carlsbad and were in the mountains now, but not under any circumstances they could have predicted.

She looked at Amy, her gaze riveted on the door of the tavern as if her life depended on the return of the man they had both watched walk inside. Lucinda felt ill with the weight of all that had happened since she and Devon had last been in bed. Now she didn't know if she would ever want him to touch her again, or how, without his support, she could help Amy through what lay ahead. Because Lucinda had guessed the meaning behind his ambiguous answers: he didn't believe Nathan was alive. If that turned out to be true, Amy would need more than platitudes to keep her afloat. She would need the wisdom of someone winnowed by a grief that cut to the bone. Lucinda knew grief, but a loss arising from an accident might be less than one intentionally inflicted. She had no experience with that.

Helplessly watching her daughter's undaunted faith in a man she felt had misled them, Lucinda quietly slid out of his truck, closing the door just to the point that the latch didn't catch but the dome light was off. Hugging herself in the cold wind, she didn't go far, not wanting to leave Amy alone. But it felt good to move, so she paced back and forth. On one of her turns she saw Devon come out of the tavern. As she watched him approach, she knew he had seen her though she couldn't read his eyes. It was too dark and he was too far away.

He stopped at the truck and opened the door. She watched him turn off the light, then speak to Amy, though she couldn't hear their words above the soughing wind in the trees. Amy leaned forward so he could get something from behind the seat. Silhouetted against the light from the tavern, it looked like a tightly rolled sleeping bag and maybe a blanket. He gave the bag to Amy, then quietly closed the door and brought the blanket to her. Accepting it, she saw it was a serape. As she gratefully enclosed herself in the wool's warmth, she busied herself longer than necessary settling the unfamiliar garment on her shoulders.

"Buck's visiting in the cabin," Devon said softly. "I'd like to stay and follow him in the morning, but I'll take you home if that's what you want."

"You could do that and be back by dawn," she said.

"I guess that's an answer," he said, turning away.

"Wait," she whispered, half hoping he wouldn't hear so the trip home would be set in motion.

But he turned around and waited.

Amy was out of sight, probably snuggled in his bag, maybe already asleep. She looked at Devon and said helplessly, "Talk to me."

He took her hand and led her across the road to where a fallen tree was lodged in front of a boulder, affording a natural seat on the dark edge of the forest. "Let me help keep you warm," he murmured, as if that were his only motive for holding her close as they sat on the log.

She could feel the stock of his gun poking into her shoulder, as well as the strength of his arms. Tilting her head back to see he was watching the cabin across the empty, moonlit road, she tried to sound playful when she said, "This is my first stakeout."

He chuckled. "I've been on lots of 'em." He gave her a smile. "But never in such good company."

"You can never go back to it, you know that, don't you?"

He nodded, watching the cabin again.

She sat up away from him. "So it was wrong what you did, wasn't it?"

He studied her a moment, then resumed watching the cabin.

"What did you accomplish?"

"Not much."

"You're a murderer!" she whispered. "I can't believe I ever let you touch me!"

He winced. "Sorry."

"Did the man you kill have a family?"

"Yes."

"Did you tell *them* you're sorry?"

"No. If you're not gonna be quiet, we may as well leave before you wake the whole town."

"I'm whispering. Anyway, I don't care about the town. I only care about how I feel."

"It's my past. All you can do is accept it or not. Either way there's no sense fighting about it 'cause it can't be changed."

"There's sense in discussing it! You paint yourself in such a self-righteous light, as if you acted only to rid the world of one more piece of scum. But you also said he betrayed you, so there's an element of revenge in what you did, and I don't know if I want to live with a man who takes his revenge with a gun!" She stopped, then amended herself. "I don't know if I want him in my life, to say nothing of Amy's."

"I know."

"You know what?"

"How you feel, and I'm sorry I'm not the man you thought. But if I was, I wouldn't be the man I am." He smiled. "That's a song by Lyle Lovett."

"In the middle of this, you quote lyrics at me?"

"I once arrested a man while Marty Robbins was singing 'El Paso.' " He smiled again. "I like music. Don't you?"

She looked away, thinking he definitely wasn't the man she had thought.

"Oh come on, Lucinda. I fucked up bad. I paid the price and I'll keep on paying it for the rest of my life. Even so, I'm not completely sorry I did it. I was drinking pretty heavy back then and it clouded my thinking, but he was a sleazy son of a bitch who betrayed the people he'd sworn to protect. My only true regret is I didn't take his boss down with him."

Astonished she hadn't suspected a sordid cause behind his sobriety, she murmured, "So that's why you don't drink."

"I was wondering if you'd noticed."

"Being as we never went out, it wasn't real obvious."

He glanced at her, then looked back at the cabin.

"Besides," she said, "we were together too early in the day for anyone but an alcoholic to be drinking."

"Don't most people drink before sex?"

"It'd been so long since I had any, I don't know what most people do."

He smiled. "You must have a natural talent to be as good as you are when you're out of practice."

She marveled that he had led their conversation from an accusation of murder to a compliment on sex. Though she conceded her criticism concerned his past, she also knew her acceptance wouldn't be a finite decision but an ongoing reality, imbuing fear into every knock on her door. She was about to tell him that when he shushed her by smothering her face against his chest. She twisted free to follow his gaze to the cabin where she could just barely discern the silhouette of a man on the porch. They watched him emerge from the shadows, moonlight glinting off his blond hair as he walked to the Pontiac. Its engine sounded like a locomotive in the quiet village, then settled down to only a roar when he put it in gear. The headlights swung across her and Devon, making him duck to hide his eyes. Within the cocoon of their faces buried in his serape, she felt safe, though in an instant the illusion was gone.

"Let's go," he said, on his feet before the Pontiac's taillights disappeared around the curve heading east.

Chapter Fourteen

At the intersection of 82 and 285 in Artesia, Buck decided against turning south. He hated the Pontiac and wanted to be rid of it bad, but didn't figure he'd gain anything by changing cars with a cop on his tail. The fucker must've followed him to Mayhill 'cause as soon as he opened the throttle on a straightaway coming back, he'd seen the Dodge pickup with the same three heads in his rearview mirror. What kind of cop took a woman and kid on a manhunt? It didn't make sense, but that they were following him couldn't be denied. His only consolation was they hadn't had time to question Russ in the cabin and still be so hot on his tail.

He tried to remember everything he'd told Russ. They were drinking beer the whole time, and as near as Buck could recall their conversation had meandered from memories of their days as cellmates to the likelihood of the Braves winning the pennant. Past and future, in other words, with not much wasted on the present. Russ was lucky to have inherited that cabin. He cut wood in season for a contractor, picked up a few odd cowboying jobs, and otherwise ate off his EBT card. If Buck owned a place, he could do the same, but having to ante up a couple hundred for rent every month would put the pinch on anyone without a steady income. That's why he'd gone along with this payback scheme for his cousin. Zeb stood to inherit millions. To be in his good graces ought to be worth something.

Buck couldn't see the Dodge in his rearview, so when the

light changed he scurried through the intersection and pulled into the Diamond Shamrock across from the Navajo Refinery. Unable to drive behind the building, he parked at an angle nosed toward the back, as far out of sight as he could manage. Inside he used the payphone to call Zeb's private line.

It rang twice, then he could hear Zeb breathing.

"It's me," Buck said, hunching against the wall.

After a moment, Zeb whispered, "You shouldn't be calling me now."

"Is it that late?"

"It's midnight, asshole. What do you want?"

He sniffed, trying hard not to take offense. "I'm pretty close. I thought I might go by."

"Here?"

"Where we left him."

He heard the rustle of what sounded like bedding before Zeb asked, "Why?"

Buck shrugged. "Just to check."

"Are you going to buy him the Coke you were supposed to bring me in the cemetery? Maybe take along a Big Mac and fries?"

"What's the matter, Zeb? Why're you being so mean?"

"The cops're all over me. They may even have this phone tapped."

He felt a clammy sweat on the back of his neck. "They questioned you?"

"Twice. So I don't think this call is a good idea."

"How'd they know to come to you?"

"The school secretary helped an artist draw a sketch of the kidnapper." Zeb laughed. "It wasn't very flattering, but somehow they figured out we're cousins."

"They got a picture of me?"

"It's actually a drawing. Did you get rid of the car?"

"Not yet."

"What're you waiting for?"

"There's a cop on my tail. I've been trying to lose him first."

"That's why you shouldn't go back. The only reason he hasn't already arrested you is he's hoping you'll lead him there."

"He's not a real cop. I think he's on vacation or something."

"Then how do you know he's a cop?"

"I can tell. Listen, Zeb, you gonna give me some money when this is over?"

"If you stay out of jail. If you don't, you won't need any."

"I'll need a lawyer."

"That can be arranged."

"Yeah? The famous one up in Ruidoso?"

"If you keep your mouth shut."

Buck turned around and saw the Dodge parked in front of the refinery across the street. The pickup was tucked inside a dark shadow, but he could see the truck was empty. "I gotta go."

"Good idea." Zeb hung up, leaving Buck with an empty line.

He moved his mouth, pretending to talk in case the clerk was watching while his eyes searched for the cop or the girl and her mother.

Next to the Diamond Shamrock was a small restaurant called the Desert Café. Devon was inside its men's room, having left the women with their drinks at the counter. He had let them go first, hoping Buck would split while they were in the ladies' so he could leave them behind out of necessity.

But Buck's conversation had lasted longer than the women were gone, so Devon took a chance that he, too, could relieve himself before they resumed criss-crossing the southeastern corner of New Mexico in the dark of night.

Dull with fatigue, Lucinda was drinking her second cup of coffee in the hope it would give her enough energy to compensate for the fact that she would soon need another bathroom. She was beginning to wish they were home. Initially she had thought the chase was the best antidote to Amy's tearing herself apart with worry, but that theory had been worn thin by the time Amy declared she could feel Nathan behind her as they ascended into the mountains. Now they were back in the valley, and far from being drained of impetus, Amy had been so energized by her nap that her mind was tumbling through emotions Lucinda felt too weary to accommodate.

Having ordered her Coke to go, Amy had carried it over to the window where she now stood looking across the parking lot to the brightly-lit Diamond Shamrock. She couldn't see Buck inside, but she had been watching since coming out of the ladies' room and she hadn't seen him leave.

She sensed Nathan nearby. When she concentrated she could hear the quiet dripping and feel something dark and sticky, definitely dangerous, like a pool of quicksand or tar capable of trapping someone. She kept these impressions to herself. Neither her mother nor Devon had believed she could feel Nathan behind her, so she couldn't see any sense in telling them this. She merely stood at the window sipping her Coke through a straw and watching the gas station across the way.

She kept remembering the time she had spent with Buck in Zeb's car at the Sonic. It wasn't until after he was gone and Zeb told her Buck had been in prison that she saw him differently from everyone else. He didn't have a car or a job, but that wasn't unusual for kids who had graduated a few years ahead of her class. Since the oil business was in a slump, jobs were scarce unless you wanted to work in the fields. Most Anglos thought they were too good for that, so a lot of them were unemployed. And that night in Zeb's car, Buck had been talking about a book he was reading. Amy couldn't remember the title, but the fact that he would read anything he didn't have to made her think he was smart.

In the Denny's in Carlsbad, when she had walked behind him on her way to the bathroom, she had picked up that he felt afraid but not that he was dangerous. She figured he probably remembered her as well as she did him, and maybe he had liked her a little that night at the Sonic, maybe thought she was something for being with Zeb. If she was right and Zeb was behind the kidnapping, Buck might open up to her at least enough to say where Nathan was.

Refusing to think about the bad things that could happen, Amy turned away from the window and tried to walk casually past her mother toward the bathrooms. She met Devon coming out. As she brushed by him in the narrow hall, she murmured, "He's still there. I'll just be a minute."

She felt him watching so she went on into the ladies' room then waited, hoping he wouldn't be there when a moment later she looked out. The hall was empty. Quietly she walked to the door at the other end. Outside, she ran across the lot and behind the Diamond Shamrock to where the Pontiac was parked. She opened a back door and got in.

Crouching on the floor so no one could see her, she was overwhelmed with the sensation of Nathan's presence. She felt nauseous and could smell the carpet as if it were against her face. The sickening sensation was so strong she was torn between wanting to escape and clinging to a place where Nathan had been. When she had almost convinced herself to get out, she heard the driver's door open and felt a new presence that felt sharp and mean and made her huddle close to the floor. She heard the key in the ignition, then the engine. The transmission shifted into reverse and the wheels turned. They stopped as if to give her one last chance, but she was too late. As she fumbled for the door handle, she looked out the window and saw Devon running toward her. Then the transmission shifted again, and this time when the wheels turned, they were on the highway picking up speed.

Devon had been on his feet, antsy with pent-up energy. Having already paid for their drinks, he was impatient to be back at the truck and ready to leave as soon as Buck did. Amy, however, was taking her time in the bathroom. He looked at Lucinda, wondering if she had noticed anything amiss in her daughter, but he didn't ask, feeling she should be the one to break the silence that had settled between them.

"I'll be at the truck," he said, making the decision an instant before the words came out of his mouth.

She looked at him so long he wondered if she was hoping he would leave them behind. The motel they had discussed earlier was an easy walk from the café, and he would feel comfortable letting them make that walk if Buck was in sight. As it was, he couldn't even see the Pontiac and had only Amy's word that Buck hadn't left.

"I'll get Amy," Lucinda said, tucking her purse under her arm as she rose to her feet.

She looked tired, so he waited, watching the parking lot as he rattled his keys in his pocket. The café was empty so late at night, and he took a smidgeon of pleasure from the metallic rhythm he kept going until he saw Lucinda come back, her face distorted with distress.

"She's not there!" she cried.

He tossed her the keys. "Get the truck," he said, already pushing through the door.

He ran across the parking lot and turned the corner on the Diamond Shamrock in time to catch the Pontiac backing up. Seeing Amy peek out from the back seat, he felt the door handle beneath his fingertips as the car shot forward. He ran a few steps after it, then stopped, hearing his truck fishtail across the oil-slick lot. He jumped in on the passenger side while the truck was still moving.

"Floor it," he told Lucinda.

The Pontiac's taillights were specks ascending a distant ridge as she sped onto the highway.

"Is Amy with him?"

"I saw her in the backseat."

"Oh my God," she whimpered.

"Don't cry! Keep your eyes on the road."

They crested the ridge and saw the taillights below. Lucinda couldn't give the pickup more gas, the accelerator was already flat on the floor, but she hunched closer to the wheel as if that would help. Devon rolled down his window and pulled his Beretta from its shoulder holster.

"You can't shoot!" she wailed. "Amy'll be hurt!"

"Maybe not, if I hit a tire."

"Maybe's not good enough! How'd he get her in his car?"

"She put herself there."

"I can't believe that!"

"Did you see him come into the café and take her?"

She shook her head. "Is a gun your typical solution to problems?"

It took him a minute before he conceded, "Sometimes I leave town."

"Is that what you'll do when you've finished with us?"

180

He watched her staring straight ahead as if she could see Amy inside the station wagon, but it was too far away.

"I haven't been feeling real welcome," he said.

"Even in these circumstances," she muttered, "it's hard to welcome a man with a gun."

He slid the Beretta back in its holster and snapped it closed. "Don't let up. I think we're gaining on him."

Amy huddled on the floor, not having anticipated a high-speed chase. She had thought she could talk to Buck there in the parking lot, and she felt sorry now to think of how scared her mother must be. Also that Devon might use his gun to get her back. Maybe he would kill Buck, and the fact that he had a second killing on his conscience would be her fault. She knew the first one bothered him, no matter how macho he tried to be about it. Another might be his undoing. Even worse would be if the only person who knew Nathan's whereabouts died before telling anyone. Determined not to let that happen, she slowly pulled herself up to sit on the seat.

Buck's eyes in the rearview mirror were scared, and she could see that the speedometer read over ninety. The desert whipped by in a blur. Looking over her shoulder, she saw headlights in the distance. She wished she could tell Devon to slow down, that she was okay and probably would be if Buck didn't wreck his car because he was going too fast. She turned around and watched him in the mirror.

Buck thought he heard something in the back seat. Telling himself it was impossible, he looked in the mirror and saw bright blue eyes meeting his. He nearly jumped out of his skin before realizing it was the girl.

"Hi," she said with a funny little smile.

The car swerved across the center line then skirted the

shoulder before he managed to get it under control without breaking speed. He concentrated on the tunnel of light his headlights were carving while he tried to figure what the girl was doing there.

The ice in her Coke rattled as she climbed over the seat. Intending to lean against the door, she pushed its button down just as Buck shouted, "Don't lock it!"

"Why not?"

" 'Cause now I gotta use pliers to get it open, dipshit, and I don't have any. Do you?"

She shook her head and faced him with her back to the door as she sipped her Coke through the straw.

He looked at her Coke. "Can I have some of that?"

She held it toward him. "I already drank most of it."

He took the cup and sucked on the straw till nothing came out, then gave the cup back as the road ducked into a gully. He put both hands on the wheel and stepped on the brake. The car skidded. He yanked the emergency brake so the car swung around, flinging her against the door. The highway they had just traveled was in front of her now, the car nosed toward a dirt road into the dunes.

She looked for Devon's headlights, but the rise of the gully blocked her view. Realizing the blind worked both ways, she unrolled her window while pushing one sneaker off with her other foot. Buck gunned the engine, catapulting the car into the dunes. Watching him concentrate on the dirt road in front of them, she threw her shoe and the cup toward the pavement. He turned off the lights and drove with only the moon to show the way. The car's interior was dark, but she caught a gleam from the whites of his eyes when he said, "I wanted that ice."

"I didn't know," she said.

He watched the road, so she did too: pale caliche between

thickets of mesquite, dark shrubs with three-inch thorns. His voice sharper than before, he asked, "What're you doing here?"

"I wanted to talk to you." She swallowed, gathering courage. "Do you remember me?"

"Yeah, sure. You're the girl got raped."

"What?"

"That's why we took Nathan, to pay him back. Otherwise I wouldn't be in this mess."

"Zeb told you Nathan raped me?"

"The whole school knows. He wasn't telling any secrets."

"All that's a secret to me!"

"What d'ya mean?"

"It never happened! Zeb lied!"

Buck stared at her so long the car went off the road, the mesquite thorns shrieking against its sides. After swerving back on track, he pounded the wheel with his fists and yelled, "Goddamn sonofabitch!" He stepped hard on the accelerator, bouncing the car over the washboard road, careening into the thickets as often as not.

"You're gonna wreck your car!" she shouted.

"Like it's worth saving!" he shouted back. "This's what I get for taking a kidnapping rap and getting sent back to prison. A lousy car ain't worth shit!"

But he eased off so their ride wasn't as frantic, just a swashbuckling meander through the sands. She looked at the looming dunes—pale hummocks speckled with greasewood and grama grass bending in the wind.

"You said you wanted to talk to me," he growled. "How come you're not saying nothing?"

"I guess I'm scared."

"You got good reason."

"I don't believe you'll hurt me."

"You don't know anything about me, little girl. Were you even dating Nathan Wheeler?"

"He's my boyfriend."

"So Zeb did all this 'cause he was jealous of that four-eyed cadet?"

"Did all *what*?"

He stared straight ahead.

Softly she pleaded, "Will you tell me where he is?"

"Home in bed. I called him at that Shamrock. Know what he said? That I shouldn't call him no more!"

"No, I mean Nathan. Where Nathan is."

"You don't want to go there."

"Yes, I do."

He reached across and grabbed her hair, pulling her face close when he snarled, "No, you don't."

"You're hurting me," she whimpered.

He threw her back against the door. "You try getting out and if I don't run you down with the car, I'll shoot you."

She sniffled. "I don't see a gun."

"I got one, though, so don't go thinking I don't like a minute ago you was thinking I wouldn't hurt you. That wasn't true, was it?"

"No," she said.

"You tell *me* something. What's that cop doing on my tail all night? And don't tell me he ain't a cop 'cause I can smell the goddamn fuckers."

"We're looking for Nathan."

"You must think I'm stupid, expecting me to lead you there."

"I was hoping we could take him something to eat."

He snorted. "Zeb was talking about that a minute ago."

"Let's do it, you and me."

He smiled, his teeth flashing white. "Zeb told me not to."

"Fuck Zeb."

He laughed. "That's what he wants to do to you."

"Doesn't he do it to everyone? Isn't that what he's done to you?"

"I ain't no fag!"

"I meant metaphorically."

"You think I don't know that word, don'cha? Think I'm dumb, huh? I used to go to a school like yours. Everything that happens inside 'em is shit. What do you think of that?"

"I don't think you're dumb. Remember when I was with Zeb at the Sonic and you came and sat in his car? You were talking about some book you were reading, and I thought you were smart!"

He frowned. "That was you?"

Her heart sank, realizing her didn't remember her.

"You like me?" he sneered.

"I could," she said bravely.

"Maybe I'll just stop up here a ways and find out how much."

Amy knew then that she had made a terrible mistake.

Chapter Fifteen

Pete Reck sat in the interrogation room, feeling his first suspicion that this arrest wasn't like the others he'd endured. It was too late in the night for a frivolous questioning, and the detective facing him across the table looked too solemn for the petty crimes Pete habitually committed.

The detective's name was Saavedra. Dark and built like an inverted triangle, he looked ready to doubt every answer Pete gave.

"What were you doing at that house?"

"Just looking."

"For what?"

"Nothing."

Saavedra reached across the table and slapped him. "Try again."

He blinked back tears, knowing he was in deep shit if the detective felt no qualms about roughing him up. Not that he hadn't been worked over by cops before, but that had been uniformed patrolmen on the street, not undercover dicks inside the precinct. "I was just looking 'cause nobody answered the door."

"That usually means no one's home and you're s'posed to go away."

"I didn't do nothing."

"Then why were you there?"

"I wanted to talk to her."

"Who?"

"The librarian lady."

"What librarian lady?"

"Lucinda Sterling's her name. I just wanted to talk to her."

"What about?"

He looked away from the detective's hard eyes. "It's personal."

"You want to know personal, how about I step on your balls? Would that be personal enough?"

"I haven't done anything! What is it you think I've done?"

"Tell me what you wanted to talk to Mrs. Sterling about."

"I wanted to thank her!"

"For what?"

"Being nice! Is that a crime?"

Saavedra shook his head. "Do you own a car?"

"Yeah, I carry my pack around 'cause I don't want to get the seat dirty."

Saavedra slapped him again. "I'm trying to impress on you, son, that I'm serious here."

"I'm not your son!"

"Okay, kid, buster, pal, buddy, whatever the hell you wanta be called."

"I want to be called Mr. Reck."

"When I'm talking to the media, I'll call you mister, right now you're *pendejo*. You know what that means?"

"A son of a bitch," he mumbled.

"That's right. How long've you known Buck Powell?"

"Never heard of him."

"How about Zeb Mulroney?"

Pete shook his head.

"Amy Sterling? Ever hear of her?"

"Is she related to Lucinda?"

"Do you know her?"

"I know Mrs. Sterling from the library. She was nice when

most folks ain't. I'm leaving town tomorrow and wanted to thank her, that's all."

"Where you going?"

"Florida."

"How you gonna get there?"

"Hitch."

Saavedra stared in sullen silence before finally saying, "You're not going anywhere tomorrow."

"I didn't do nothing!"

"Trespassing with intent to break and enter. That's worth at least thirty days."

"No, man. I was just looking through the window, thinking what a pretty house it was and how nice it'd be to live there and all."

"Ever hear of a kid named Nathan Wheeler?"

Pete shook his head. "What'd he do, get murdered or something?"

"What makes you say that?"

"Oh no," Pete moaned. "You can't pin a murder on me just 'cause I was looking in a window."

"Are you saying he was murdered?"

"I don't even know who you're talking about."

The door opened and another cop came in, this one blond and pudgy. "What d'ya say, Alex, want me to work him over?"

Pete felt dread blanket his fear. "Come on, guys. I'm just a drifter passing through."

Saavedra stood up. "Let's leave him to think about it a while."

Hearing the lock catch, Pete felt trapped as he watched his reflection in the two-way mirror.

It looked like a beacon in the road ahead. Not where a beacon should be, alongside or above the highway, the small strip of reflected light lay in the middle of the lane they were traveling, enough of an anomaly that they both studied it in silence as they approached.

The road stretched flat all the way to Texas, and except for them, it was apparently empty. So when Lucinda spotted the object, she eased up on the accelerator. An anomaly, after all, had a better chance of providing a clue than nothing.

She allowed the pickup to move more and more slowly as the object came into definition. It assumed the shape of a tiny triangle missing its top, then suggested two horseshoes holding their luck, one above the other. Recognizing a sneaker that had landed right side up, reflectors on its heel to protect a person who ran in the dark, she stopped the truck.

Devon watched her walk into the beam of headlights to stare down at the shoe. Looking far ahead, he saw the lights of a vehicle approaching from the very edge of the horizon. He leaned across to close the driver's door, then got out on the passenger side and joined her where she stood in the head-lights, cradling the sneaker against her breasts.

Searching for anything that might be connected, he saw something white in a withered stand of prickly clover: a cup with the same design used in the Desert Café. Lucinda moaned. He watched her slowly sink to her knees, her head bowed over the shoe she held as if it were a living thing in need of comfort. He kept his distance, trying to piece the clues together, until he heard the rumble of an eighteen-wheeler coming fast.

The truck was on top of them sooner than he'd antici-pated, its horn blasting a warning above the roar of its engine. He lifted Lucinda to her feet and pulled her off the pavement as the wind of the trailer's passing fluttered their clothes like flags in a gust of sand. She sobbed against his chest, the shoe between them a lump lodged below his breastbone. In the ensuing quiet, he leaned his face close and deciphered the mangled words escaping her throat.

"It's Amy's." Her shoulders shook with her sobs, as if her daughter's loss of a shoe meant she had lost her daughter.

He looked over the top of her head as he listened to the wind move the cup in the clover, its thorns scraping like fingernails picking at cardboard. Almost directly in front of him a dirt road led into the dunes of Mescalero Sands. "Look, Lucinda!" He turned her around to see for herself. "She threw the shoe out to tell us he left the highway."

"Do you think . . . ?" she whimpered.

He guided her to his truck, helped her in, then took the wheel. Together they drove off the pavement heading north, back toward Berrendo.

The dunes were a sixty-mile stretch of aeolian sand accumulated over eons under Mescalero Ridge. The crusted hummocks were peppered with dark-spined lechugia, scraggly white button flowers, and spindly scrub oaks swaying in the beam of his headlights when he turned off one dirt track onto another, all of them washboard caliche swept by the wind. Lucinda held the shoe to her breasts as if it were a favorite toy from her daughter's childhood.

As each mile passed with no sight of the Pontiac, Devon felt his hope dim with the failing light of the setting moon. He fought the dread of defeat, buoying his hope by staying alert for any change, no matter how subtle. But the only discernable difference was the gradual arrival of dawn.

It was six A.M. and Jane Dorrie was waiting at the police station to speak with the detective in charge of the Nathan Wheeler case. She sat primly on a plastic chair outside the interrogation rooms, her red curls flounced on her shoulders, her green eyes made up with brown shadow and thick mascara, her lithe body clothed in a snug turquoise suit luminous under the fluorescent lights.

Alex Saavedra stood behind the tiny window in the otherwise solid door, wondering what had motivated the secretary to turn against her boss. He felt sure that was why she had come—to share some tidbit of incriminating conversation overheard in Mulroney's law office—and the likelihood that she was jeopardizing her job by being here hadn't stopped her.

She was lovely, polished and lustrous, while he had been wearing the same clothes for twenty-four hours and needed a shave as well as a shower. So he hesitated, made more keenly aware of his grunge by contemplating her beauty. Reminding himself his sex appeal wasn't at issue, he opened the door and invited her in, wishing the room could be fancier but knowing she needed the security of absolute privacy.

She walked like water rippling over rocks, though a tiny tic above the left corner of her mouth betrayed how nervous she felt. He gestured for her to sit in the chair he had occupied while questioning Pete Reck a few hours before. Too dirty to comfortably get any closer, he closed the door and leaned against it, contenting himself with the fact that at least he didn't have bugs, which wasn't something he could say for sure about Reck.

"You'll excuse me if I keep my distance," he apologized with a wry smile. "I've been here all night and feel kinda ripe."

When she looked up and smiled, a tiny spark ignited between them, but he didn't guess such a luscious woman would harness her wagon to a detective's salary.

She didn't jump right into whatever she had come here to say, so he offered, "Can I get you some coffee?"

"No, thank you." She smiled again, fanning the spark to a flame.

He tried to ignore it, knowing some women could only approach authority by playing the coquette, also suspecting any woman who worked for Silas Mulroney had been hired at least partially as a courtesan.

"This is difficult," she murmured. "You can understand my hesitation."

He waited.

"I wouldn't be here," she said, "except that I feel so badly for the boy who was taken. I have a nephew his age." She paused to give him a smile. "My brother's considerably older than I am."

Saavedra nodded, politely accepting the implication that she was far too young to have a teenage son herself.

"I was awake all night, thinking of how I'd feel if this were happening to my family, so I decided I had to come tell you what I know."

He waited, wanting to hear it exactly as she chose to phrase it.

"Yesterday," she began, "Mrs. Mulroney came to the office very upset."

He raised his eyebrows, encouraging her to continue.

"I couldn't help overhear." She stopped again. "No, that's not true. I deliberately eavesdropped."

He smiled, and to his surprise a tinge of color lit her cheeks, as if he and she were fencing in a smoky nightclub.

She took a deep breath, pushing what was happening between them into the background as she confessed, "There's a bathroom off Mr. Mulroney's office. I went in there and listened through the tile wall of the shower."

"I'm glad you did."

"It's not something I usually do, I want you to understand that."

He nodded.

"I heard her say their son and his cousin kidnapped Nathan Wheeler from school."

"Their son?" he asked, needing a name.

"Zebediah Mulroney the Second. You know—Li'l Zeb?"

"And the cousin's name?"

"She just called him Buck."

"Did she say why they did it?"

"She didn't know."

He held his breath, hoping against hope. "Did she say where they took him?"

Jane shook her head.

He fought disappointment. "Anything else?"

"She said Li'l Zeb has a photo album of pictures taken of Amy when she didn't know he was taking them."

"Did she say where he kept the album?"

"In his room. She accused Mr. Mulroney of creating a monster."

"Meaning Li'l Zeb?"

She nodded, the fire now a comfortable glow of compatible coals. "Silas was beside himself. I mean, she was practically hysterical, and then at the end, she sounded so cruel. She must hate him to say something like that."

"But not his money."

She blushed.

"Are you sleeping with him?"

Her cheeks paled as she hid her eyes behind their heavy mascara.

"I only ask," he lied, "because if you are and you testify in court, the defense could suggest an ulterior motive."

"I've told you the truth!"

"I'm sure you have. Will you testify?"

"I'd lose my job."

"And your bed partner."

She stared at him, their flirtation dead.

"Think about it," he said with resignation. "It may turn out we don't need you." He forced a professional kindness into his voice as he opened the door. "Whether we do or not, I appreciate your coming forward."

She stood up but otherwise didn't move.

"Is there something else?"

Coquettish again, she said, "For a moment I thought . . ."

"I don't care for chewed cabbage."

Her eyes flashed, their fire angry now.

He watched her walk out, leaving behind the charred corpse of what could have been a delicious seduction.

Silas knocked on the door of Old Zeb's home office, then stepped in with a bright smile and asked, "No kind word of greeting for your only son, Father?"

From behind his mammoth ebony desk, Zeb barked, "I didn't invite you here at seven o'clock in the morning to shower you with endearments!"

"When have you ever?" Silas took a cigar from his pocket and held it beneath his nose.

"Don't light that!"

"I know you can't tolerate tobacco anymore. You smoked too many of Castro's finest when they were illegal to be able to enjoy them now that they're not."

"You're a despicable son of a bitch."

"If you insist on insulting my mother, I'll have to leave."

"You'll go when I say so! You're only here 'cause of your son."

"You mean your grandson and heir?"

"I mean Li'l Zeb! What the hell's he into?"

"Why don't you ask him?"

"I did. Now I'm asking you."

"Apparently he kidnapped a boy from school. That's all I know about it."

Zeb glowered at his son sniffing the cigar, a perfume denied him as much as women now that his heart was giving out. Other than wealth, all he had to show for his years was this insignificant fop of a son and a grandson who was starting out on what anyone would call an extremely wrong foot. "Ambrose tells me you let the police question Li'l Zeb without an attorney."

"I was there."

"What'd he tell 'em?"

"Only that the girl involved will be unable to put out for Nathan in the future."

"Who is she?"

"Just a schoolgirl."

"Li'l Zeb's sweet on her?"

"I hesitate to say he's capable of being sweet on anyone."

Old Zeb listened to the mantle clock tick away the increasingly finite minutes of his life. "Why do you always stymie me?"

"Do I?" Silas answered, pleased at the thought.

"Even when you were a tyke, you'd cry every time I came into a room."

"Perhaps because you hit me every time."

"For your own good! You were always misbehaving."

"Do you think you taught me well?"

The old man spit into the brass receptacle beside his desk. "Don't hate my money, though, do you?"

"I haven't seen any of your money since I graduated from law school."

"Your wife has."

"Yes, well, we're not what you'd call close."

"What'd you marry her for? I told you not to!"

"She was pregnant, remember? And Mother said the Church forbade abortion."

"That doesn't mean you marry every chippie you knock up!"

"Alicia was the daughter of a respectable family. They threatened a paternity suit."

"You should've let 'em sue."

"Mother forbade it."

"Mother forbade it, the Church forbade it. Why didn't you listen to what I told you?"

"We weren't speaking at the time."

"But I let you know what I wanted!"

"Through a letter from Ambrose, yes, you did." He returned the cigar to the inside pocket of his jacket. "All that's irrelevant now. I thought you'd grown to like Alicia."

"I do," the old man mumbled. "And I love your son."

"So I haven't been a total disappointment."

"Goddamn it, boy! I tried to love you."

"Let's get to the point: What are we going to do about your namesake?"

"Protect him."

"Even if it means throwing Cousin Buck to the wolves?"

"Do you think Zeb would've done it without him?"

"I don't think Buck would have done it without Zeb."

"Which proves Buck's pliable. According to Ambrose, if the Wheeler boy comes home safe, Buck shouldn't be sentenced to more'n ten years. We can promise him Easy Street when he's out. That oughta keep him quiet."

"If Nathan comes home safe."

"A little roughin' up never hurt a boy."

"Apparently, in your estimation, neither does a lot."

Chapter Sixteen

Amy lay on her side with her butt nestled in the spoon of Buck's groin, both of his arms around her waist as he snored against the nape of her neck. After driving for what seemed like hours the night before, he had stopped in this arroyo between dunes and announced they would spend the night.

"Why?" she had blurted out.

" 'Cause I'm tired. What'd you think? We'd go to a motel?"

She shook her head. "Do you have two sleeping bags?"

"I don't even have a blanket, little girl. We're gonna have to keep each other warm."

He got out, opened the back door and flipped the seat to lay flat. "Climb over," he said, "unless you gotta pee or something?"

Reluctantly she crawled into the back of the station wagon.

"What happened to your shoe?"

"I lost it."

"When?"

"I don't know. In the mountains, I think."

"Well, stretch out. I ain't gonna sleep sitting up."

She lay down as far from him as she could get.

He got in and closed the door, then lay on his side facing her, though it was so dark she could barely see him. When she felt him pull her close, she struck out blindly, flailing with her hands and feet.

"Quit it!" he shouted. "I ain't gonna do nothing. Roll on your side with your back to me so we can sleep like hobos." He positioned her the way he wanted, then locked his arms around her waist to hold her tight. "If you try'n get away, I'll beat the shit outta you."

She didn't say anything, believing him.

After a moment, he said, "Your hair smells good."

She squeezed her eyes shut, remembering how often Nathan had told her that. Trying not to cry, she asked, "Won't you take me to Nathan? I'll help you if you do. I'll tell the police you didn't hurt me when you could've, and you took me there before it was too late."

"Go to sleep."

"I don't think I can, knowing he's cold and hungry and all alone."

"Nobody's ever all alone. The universe is full of demons. Didn't you know that?"

She took no comfort from his words. When his steady breathing told her he was asleep, she reminded herself that Nathan had been in this car not long ago. She concentrated on trying to conjure whatever remnant he may have left in the hope she could glean a hint of his location, but her senses were overwhelmed by the clammy presence of the man pressed against her from behind. Angrily she jabbed her elbow into him.

He grunted, then snuffled awake.

"Why won't you take me to Nathan? Why can't we sleep there?"

" 'Cause it's wet."

"What do you mean?"

"There was a leaky pipe. The floor's all wet."

Her heart leapt as she remembered hearing the drip of water. "If he's wet, he'll be cold."

"We gave him a coat. Now shut up and go to sleep."

"You gave him a coat?"

"Well, it was more like a cloak."

"That was nice of you."

"Yeah, right. We're real nice. If you don't go to sleep, I'm gonna conk you on the head."

She kept quiet after that, clinging to the hope that in the morning she could convince him to take her to Nathan. As the night wore on, she slept fitfully, and dawn found her wide awake. Knowing that on any given Saturday someone was bound to come to the Sands—it was a popular area for motorcycles and dune buggies—she concentrated on listening beyond the rhythm of his breathing for the sound of an engine. When she heard one, her eyes flew open in the sudden awareness that she had waited too long. If she tried to slip out of his grasp, the engine's noise might penetrate his sleep and wake him. Even so, she had to try.

Lifting his fingers, she pried his hands apart, then started to slide between his palms. She managed to clear his grip, but had her back to him so couldn't stop his one hand from falling on the other. He snuffled, but didn't wake up. Still she waited, listening to his even breathing, before she started inching toward the back of the wagon. She figured he wouldn't sleep through her opening the door, so she had to move fast. If she could get out, she could outrun him, she was pretty sure of that. She was almost to the door when his hand grabbed her ankle.

"Where you going?"

"I have to pee."

Still holding onto her, he sat up, snuffled loudly a couple of times, then cleared his throat. "I'll go with you."

"Puh-leeze," she said, as if concerned with her modesty.

"You think I'm gonna let you go alone?" He bumped his

butt toward her, using only one hand to propel himself, his other hand locked on her ankle. "Go on, open the door."

She released the latch and the tailgate fell open, revealing a swatch of sand and Spanish bayonet stretching toward a freedom that wasn't yet hers.

"Let's go," he said, pushing her leg by the ankle.

She crawled to the edge of the gate, where he caught up and switched his hold to her hair, bunching it into a ponytail in his fist. He swung his legs over and stood up, then pulled her out beside him. "Let's go pee," he snickered.

She listened for the engine from before, but all she heard was a meadowlark somewhere nearby. "I don't have to anymore."

"I do."

Forced to follow him, she felt stickers prick through the sock on her shoeless foot.

He opened his trousers with his free hand. She tried not to listen to the patter on the sand, but it made her badly have to go. He zipped up his fly, then grabbed the waistband of her jeans, his fingers poking against her belly. She twisted away, but he still held her hair, so she didn't get far.

"I'm just gonna take 'em down so you don't wet your pants," he said. "I don't want you smelling like piss all day."

She sobbed as he yanked her jeans and panties down. He whacked the edge of his free hand against the back of her knees, making her fall on her butt.

"Hurry up," he growled. "I won't look."

She glanced up and saw his gaze was focused on the distance, so she raised herself to a squat and concentrated. When she was done, she stood up and pulled her clothes on as quick as she could.

"Don't you feel better?" he asked, dragging her back toward the car.

"Yes," she whimpered, trying not to cry.

"I don't know what I'm gonna do with you."

"Why don't you just let me go?"

" 'Cause if you die out here, they'll charge me with murder!" He nodded at her astonishment. "Things ain't never simple once a crime's been committed. Everything gets real complicated after that."

"Why don't you take me to Nathan? You could leave me there and I could help him, then things would get better, not worse."

He sniffed and stared at the car as he thought aloud. "I can't take you to El Paso 'cause it's across a state line and they'll charge me with rape even if I ain't done nothing."

"Leave me here. I can walk to the road. I'll be all right."

He shook his head. "Maybe I *should* put you with Nathan."

"Oh yes, please."

He leered at her. "It's dark and cold and so far out in the country you could scream your head off and nobody'd hear you. Eventually you'll starve to death, and when someday they decide to tear the building down or maybe use it for something and find you, all you'll be is bones."

She sank to her knees in the sand.

He shook her by her hair. "I don't want to hurt you, but I can't think what else to do!"

"Ow!" she cried, holding her scalp with both hands.

Then she saw his face. He was listening. She forced herself to be quiet so she could hear too: an engine, not far away. "Help!" she screamed, her feet digging frantic troughs as she tried to stand up. "Help me!"

"Shut up!" he bellowed, punching her mouth with his fist.

She fell backwards and he let go. Her vision a swirl of red, she drove her feet into his groin. He let out a gust of breath, crumpling to his knees as she scrambled to her feet and ran toward the engine she could hear just beyond the next dune.

She started to yell again for help, but when she saw the familiar brown pickup, the word that came out of her mouth was "Mom!" as she catapulted toward the truck's door.

It opened and she was vaguely aware of Devon running toward her, her mother behind him, then she was in her arms and they were both crying and hugging each other as if someone were trying to pull them apart.

Devon heard a car door slam just before he rounded the hummock and saw the Pontiac, Buck pumping the accelerator to start the engine. As Devon yanked the door open and dragged him out, Buck swung his fist. Devon ducked and came back with a right that slammed Buck back against the side of the car. Buck put his hands up to his face, so Devon pummeled his gut until he dropped to all fours, a spindle of blood spiraling from his mouth.

Devon pulled his pistol and aimed it at the limp blond head, forcing himself not to pull the trigger. Breathing hard, he took a step back just as the women came around the hummock. He glanced at them, allowing the awareness that Amy was safe to ease his mind, then looked back at Buck on his knees.

Amy cried, "He told me he has a gun!"

"Where?"

"I don't know."

He stepped closer to Buck. "Where is it?"

Buck crawled around to sit on his butt, his legs stretched straight, and wiped blood from his mouth before mumbling, "My left boot. Want me to get it?"

"Like hell." Devon kicked Buck hard just below his ribs.

He cried out and rolled prone, cradling his belly as Devon pulled the snub .38 out of the boot. With a gun in each hand, he retreated, then looked at the women holding onto each other, their eyes wide with a fear he didn't like seeing focused on him.

"Get my cell phone out of the truck's glove box," he said gruffly. "Call 9-1-1 and ask for the sheriff. This has gotta be his jurisdiction."

As they hurried away, Lucinda looked back over her shoulder, and he wondered if in that moment she saw him as any kind of hero.

"An abandoned building out in the country," Saavedra said in the second floor lounge of the police station. "That narrows it down to only half the universe."

Devon smiled, sympathizing with his sarcasm. "A helicopter would help."

"We got 'copters and a posse on horseback and pretty near every squad car in both counties, but it's still gonna take time to search what amounts to more'n ten thousand square miles."

"My guess is it's close to the intersection of 285 and 82, just 'cause he kept hovering around it."

Saavedra nodded, assessing the man who was only a few years older but had a lot more experience investigating homicides. "How'd you catch his tail?"

"I was lucky."

"Pretty amazing he could drive around all night when we had an APB out on the Pontiac and never laid eyes on it."

"Happens that way sometimes."

"Course it would've helped if we'd known he switched plates."

Devon kept quiet.

"From what I've heard about El Paso," Saavedra teased, "cops deal their own justice."

"You heard wrong."

"Uh-huh. And Buck got those bruises from falling down a flight of stairs, is that what you're saying?"

Devon smiled, telling Saavedra the older detective knew he wasn't about to be arrested for catching a suspect two counties had made the object of a manhunt. Saavedra pulled the Beretta out of his belt and handed it over butt-first. "We checked on the registration. It's legit."

"Thanks," Devon said, returning the gun to his shoulder holster.

"What're you gonna do now?"

"Get some sleep."

"Sounds like heaven, but I can't do that till Buck tells us where the kid is." Saavedra couldn't help wondering why Devon had quit police work since he was so good at it. "My partner's grilling him now," he added, leaving an unspoken invitation dangling in the air.

Devon let it dangle.

"Chief wants to see you 'fore you go."

"You know what about?"

"Yeah, and so do you, but if I say it you might not be able to act surprised."

Devon laughed. "I don't know about surprised, but I'd probably be more polite if he'd let me get some sleep first."

"He's known for not doing that."

Chief Hudson was feeling the anxiety of nicotine withdrawal after smoking two packs back to back while falling off the wagon he'd ridden for three years. He was also unhappy that a retired cop from El Paso had caught the suspect the combined police force of two counties were unable to nab, but he felt he owed it to the citizens to at least thank the man. When he was facing the recipient of his reluctant gratitude across his cluttered desk, those thoughts were expressed and acknowledged in a staccato pattern reflecting how tired both men were.

"What'll you do now?" Hudson asked, unaware he was echoing the words of his detective.

"Get some sleep," Devon repeated as graciously as he could.

"I mean in the long run."

Devon waited.

"You ever think of wearing a badge again?"

"I think about it."

"Would you consider using your talents to protect the people of Berrendo?"

"Not as a cop."

The chief sighed. "If you don't wanta wear a badge, don't do no more police work in my jurisdiction."

"I won't," Devon promised.

But by the time he was in the parking lot under the blue sky of noon, he was wondering if Buck might have let something slip to his friend in Mayhill.

Lucinda's house was closed tight, so he figured she and Amy were asleep. He tried to be quiet going through the gate and letting himself into his apartment. After a quick shower, he was out the door again in ten minutes and had started his truck when Amy came out. She watched him as she approached along the sidewalk to stand forlornly on the curb. Sorry to see the bruise on her chin, he leaned across and opened the door, then shut off his engine when she got in.

"Where're you going?"

"To get some breakfast."

"I can cook you something."

"I don't want to be any trouble."

"You won't."

He looked down the street shaded with yellowing elms. "Where's your mother?"

"Asleep."

"I'd rather not wake her."

"Then take me with you."

"I better not."

" 'Cause I'm underage?"

He shrugged helplessly.

"The world's fucked if two people can't be friends," she said, "just 'cause one of 'em's an underage girl."

"We're friends. But if your mother woke up and found you gone, don't you think she'd be worried?"

"I can leave her a note."

He smiled. "After last night, I don't think that would help."

She stared straight ahead, though he doubted she was seeing the street. In a near whisper she asked, "Do you think they'll find Nathan in time?"

"I don't know."

"What do you *think?*"

"It's anyone's guess."

"The way Buck talked, it sounded like Nathan's still alive."

"Then he probably is."

"But you don't believe it, do you."

"It's possible."

She sighed. "Somebody named Dreyfus called." She watched him. "You're good at hiding your feelings. I couldn't see any change in you at all."

"Should there be?"

"Wasn't he your boss in El Paso?"

"Yeah."

"Aren't you worried he's tracked you here?"

"I gave him my address right after I moved in."

After a minute, she opened her door and got out. "Where'll I tell Mom you've gone?"

"Tell her I'm looking for Nathan."

Her eyes flared with accusation. "I *knew* you weren't going for breakfast. You may be good at hiding your feelings, Devon Gray, but you're an awful liar."

She slammed the door and stalked into the house without looking back.

Devon bought two Egg McMuffins and a large coffee at McDonald's before heading south. Instead of 285, he took the Y/O Ranch Road to Highway 13, which ran through Sagebrush Valley to 82. Once outside Berrendo, the prairie was so empty the only things manmade were occasional windmills. Scattered herds of pronghorn antelope watched him drive by, and he thought he saw a coyote lope across the road far in front of him, but by the time he got there, the wild dog had disappeared in an arroyo. Buzzards fluttered off the carcasses of road kill as he came close and settled back to their meal after he'd passed. The sun dropped far enough that he had to use his visor until he reached the lee of the mountains, then the air cooled fast as he drove through shade on his climb out of the valley.

Mayhill was bustling on Saturday afternoon. He counted eight people in town as he drove through to park in front of the cabin. From inside he heard a televised baseball game, but no one answered his knock for so long he was about to walk back to the tavern when finally the door opened to reveal a gangly man on the far side of thirty with a clean-shaven face under a shock of unruly black hair.

Chapter Seventeen

Having gleaned the man's name from his previous visit to the tavern, Devon introduced himself as a friend of Buck's, then said, "Your name's Russ Moore, isn't it?"

Russ nodded, looking him over before lifting the hook on the screen and pushing it open. "Come on in. You follow baseball?"

"I haven't lately, but I used to." He stepped inside and surveyed the room. What it lacked in cleanliness was made up for by the kind of comfort that only comes after decades of situating everything just right, making it look as if the room were manufactured with its clutter in place.

"I was just making coffee," Russ said. "Want some?"

"Sounds good."

Devon waited, hearing the small, homey sounds coming from the alcove kitchen just out of sight. The bedroom in back had a bath that had been tacked on long after the cabin was built, something he had noted the night before. His prior knowledge made him feel uncomfortably close to duping a man who had welcomed him in and offered him coffee. That made him realize how far he had come from being a cop, and also why, when he was one, people had usually honed in on that fact fairly fast.

Russ came out with two mugs of steaming black coffee, handed Devon one, then stood slurping at the other while watching the game. When a commercial came on, he sat down and pushed the MUTE button on the remote. "Have a seat."

Choosing a chair with a view out the front window, Devon could see the log where he and Lucinda had sat the night before. He fleetingly wished he could return to that moment when she had known only of his past violence.

"You know Buck from Santa Fe?" Russ asked.

"Berrendo."

"He never mentioned you."

"We just met last night."

Russ frowned. "We were together most of last night. I turned in kinda early, but it must've been close to midnight when I heard him leave. You saw him after that?"

Devon nodded. "In jail."

"Buck's in jail? What for?"

"He impersonated a cop to take a kid out of school."

Russ stared a moment. "He told me about the payback, but didn't say there was any kidnapping involved."

"Payback for what?"

"Raping some girl. Buck's cousin wanted her for himself, but she wasn't that kind. So when she got raped, he and Buck beat the crap outta the kid to teach him a lesson."

Devon had heard the same story from Amy. Setting his empty cup down, he said, "Zeb lied."

"You mean they got the wrong kid?"

He shook his head. "The girl wasn't raped."

"So they beat him up for nothing?"

"Maybe worse."

Russ shifted his gaze to the television, though he obviously wasn't thinking about the commercial on the screen.

Softly Devon asked, "Did Buck mention where they took the kid?"

Russ glared at him. "I can usually smell a cop. What are you, a private dick?"

"Just a friend of the family."

"Whose?"

"The girl's."

"Not Buck's."

"I'll be acting as his friend if I can find the kid alive."

Russ slowly nodded. "Yeah, I guess that's prob'ly true." He stared at the screen another minute. "I thought he was gonna stay outta jail. I really did." He stood up. "You want some more coffee?"

"Yeah," Devon said, surprised the man wasn't kicking him out.

Russ brought the pot and refilled both their cups, then returned it to the kitchen. "You used to be a cop, didn't you?" he said, sitting back down.

Devon nodded.

"Where at?"

"El Paso."

Russ snorted. "Guess you like a challenge."

Devon shrugged. "I thought I was happy there."

"So why'd you leave?"

"I couldn't keep my women straight." He smiled. "They were one problem after another."

Russ laughed. "That's all they've ever been to me."

"I walked into a situation in Berrendo that looked like it might be the end of the rainbow you stumble across when you're looking for something else. Know what I mean?"

Russ nodded. "What happened?"

"She found out I use my gun for more than target practice, so decided I'm not who she thought I was."

Russ grimaced with sympathy.

"I guess I'm not," Devon said, laying his last card on the table, "but since I'm backing out with both hands empty, I'd sure like to find the kid to prove a man adept at violence isn't totally useless in this day and age."

"This day and age," Russ scoffed, "is a glitch on the computer screen of evolution. The glitch'll pass damn quick, and then a man good at violence is gonna be valued again."

"I'm not sure that's true."

"You been talking to Buck, I can tell. But I don't believe his theory about mankind evolving to a whole new level. He gets pretty wild, doesn't he?" Russ chuckled with affection. "When he gets going on all that New Age stuff, I gotta laugh. I mean, there we were in fucking prison and he's talking about people evolving away from violence. He's reading this *Tibetan Book of the Dead* and trying to meditate while we're listening to some dude holler his head off 'cause he's getting gang-banged two cells over." Russ sipped his coffee, his face hollow. "It makes me laugh," he finished, not cracking a smile.

"Yeah," Devon mumbled.

Russ shook his head. "As to where he took the kid . . ." He looked at Devon steadily a moment, as if weighing his next words. Finally he said softly, "There used to be a tavern east of Artesia called the Cedar Crest. It's been closed a few years now."

"How far east?"

"Fifteen, twenty miles maybe? Just past Mescalero Sands."

Devon stood up. "Thanks for talking to me."

"Yeah," Russ said, standing too. "Come back anytime," he held out his hand, "long as you're not wearing a badge."

Devon smiled, shaking hands as if they were friends, which he found himself hoping they might turn out to be.

It took him two hours to retrace his path back down the eastern slope of the Sacramento Mountains and across the Pecos Valley to Artesia. He stopped for gas at the Diamond Shamrock, then drove toward Mescalero Sands.

From the top of a hill, he saw the abandoned tavern on the prairie below. Cutting his engine so his truck glided silently, he rolled across the pebbled parking lot with only the soft crunch of his tires announcing his arrival. When he opened his door and got out, the silence around the dilapidated building seemed absolute.

Knowing what he was looking for would have to be hidden from anyone traveling the road, he walked around back, his footsteps tolling a measured cadence. The tavern's rear door was open. He stepped inside, then waited for his eyes to adjust to the lesser light.

He was in a storeroom that had been emptied. Only a cardboard liquor box littered the floor, dry except for one corner where a rusted pipe dripped water in a monotonous rhythm. The passage to the tavern itself was like a tunnel into a void, cold and forbidding. A door stood barely ajar, and the scuffle marks across its threshold testified to the room's recent use.

He swung the door open. It creaked on its hinges as the diluted sunlight washed across the gray floor of what had once been a walk-in cooler. In a coagulated pool of blood a boy lay on his chest, his manacled hands secured to his bound ankles by a short length of rope. His face lay cheek down, and above his gaping mouth and broken nose, his one visible eye stared through the dull gauze of death. When Devon knelt to feel for a pulse, the flesh he touched was as cold as the concrete under his knees.

A quick survey revealed five puncture wounds in the boy's back from what could have been an ice pick, and the blood beneath his body suggested he had also been stabbed in the chest. Around his neck was a wire someone had taken the time to strip of its casing before using it as a garrote he twisted tight while the boy was already bleeding to death.

In the warmth of sunset, Devon welcomed the sweet scent of sage carried on the breeze as he walked back to his truck. He stared at the pale caprock of Mescalero Ridge while using his cell phone to call the Berrendo P.D. When Saavedra came on the line, Devon identified himself and said simply, "I found him."

"Alive?"

"No."

"Tell me where."

"The Cedar Crest Lounge east of Artesia."

"We're on our way."

Closing his eyes, he listened to the silver song of a meadowlark above the wind rustling the dry grasses until he heard the distant wail of a siren coming to take the boy home.

Parked in front of Lucinda's house was a tan Ford Taurus with Texas plates. Devon tucked his pickup behind it, then looked at the yellow house beneath the towering elms losing their leaves. In the last warmth of September the front door was open, only the screen a barrier between the world and the people inside.

He let himself in, hearing voices from the kitchen as he crossed the living room and entered the hall. On the threshold he stopped. Dreyfus sat at the table with Lucinda and Amy, all of them with half-empty coffee cups in front of them. Devon nodded at his former lieutenant, briefly met Lucinda's eyes, then knelt beside Amy's chair.

Without makeup she looked like the child she was. Yet her dark blue eyes carried a knowledge beyond years as she received the silence of his love. Suspended on that silence was a bridge she could walk only by keeping her eyes on his rather than looking down at the immense depth she might fall. Tears crowded her lashes as she met him halfway.

"Tell me," she whimpered.

"I found him."

"Alive?"

He shook his head.

The bridge held, his experience with death a path she could walk to his equally certain faith in her survival. Though tears spilled down her cheeks, she kept her balance by concentrating on the light in his eyes.

"I need to know," she whispered, "when it happened."

"Probably within an hour after they took him from school."

"So all the time we were looking for him, he was already dead?"

He nodded.

"And when I felt him so strongly behind us, he wasn't there?"

"Who knows what you felt, Amy. There's no need to deny it."

A smile trembled on her lips, a butterfly against the force of the storm, but a miracle nonetheless. Her feet now on solid ground, she stood up, looked at Dreyfus and excused herself, glanced with anguish at her mother, then left the room, sealing the moment with the soft click of the latch on her bedroom door.

Lucinda stood up just as Devon did. "Thank you," she murmured, her eyes hinting at thoughts she couldn't express before knowing her daughter was safe.

He listened to her open and close her daughter's door, then with a silent nod, invited Dreyfus outside.

In the respectful quiet surrounding a house of mourning, they followed the brick path to Devon's garage apartment. He tossed a towel into the bathroom and closed that door, then faced the lieutenant who had been his supervisor when he worked homicide in El Paso.

Dreyfus was a beefy, florid man. He stood now like an ox, his large frame out of proportion to the small room. Smiling awkwardly, he said, "You should've been a priest, Devon. Your delicacy is beyond compare."

"Have a seat. Want more coffee?"

"No thanks." He lowered his bulk onto the sofa. "Hope you don't mind my dropping by." He smiled, slightly cha-grined. "I had no idea what I was walking into."

Devon turned the wooden straight-backed chair around and straddled it backward. "I killed Ernie."

Dreyfus nodded. "Did you think I didn't know that?"

"Yeah."

"If I had my way, I'd give you a commendation for knocking him off the board."

Devon snorted in disbelief.

"I know you wouldn't accept it. I also know you must've been pushed hard to reach that point. I wish you'd come to me before you got there. Don't get me wrong: I don't care how you got rid of him, but I'm sorry as hell we lost you in the bargain."

They watched each other across the quiet room, then he asked gently, "What're you gonna do, Devon, sit in a garage and mow your landlady's lawn for the rest of your life?"

"I'm thinking of moving to the mountains."

"You'll be wasting your talents. Didn't you ever hear the story about the seed that falls on stony ground?"

Devon stood up. "Right now I'm going down to the jail and see if I can talk to their latest arrival. Want to come?"

"You bet!" Dreyfus was on his feet before Devon had tucked the wooden chair back in place.

In the lobby of the police station, Saavedra was talking to a kid wearing a backpack with a sleeping bag tied on the bottom. "Wait a minute," the detective said. "Got something for you."

He left the kid in the middle of the lobby while he went to the desk and waited for the clerk to slide an envelope through the slot under the window. When he turned around, he saw Devon standing with Dreyfus just inside the door. He gave them a quick smile, then offered the envelope to the bewildered kid. "Bus ticket to Miami," Saavedra said, "and fifty bucks for food along the way."

The kid was so astonished he couldn't bring himself to accept the envelope.

Saavedra waved it impatiently in the air. "We put the screws on you pretty hard. This is our way of saying we're sorry."

"No strings?" the kid asked suspiciously.

Saavedra stuffed the envelope in the breast pocket of the kid's filthy jacket. "Go on. Spend it in good health."

The kid took a step away, turned toward the door, then back. "Thanks."

Saavedra nodded.

Devon and Dreyfus stepped aside. After he was gone, they and Saavedra laughed softly at the kid's distrust of something good coming his way.

"What do you want?" Buck asked when he was facing Devon across the small table in the interrogation room.

"The arresting officer tells me you're gonna take the fall alone."

"What kinda shit is that? You're the arresting officer."

Devon smiled. "I don't have a badge."

"It don't seem you need one."

He glanced at the two-way mirror behind Buck's chair. "Who's watching back there?" Buck asked.

"A couple of detectives and an assistant D.A."

Without turning around, Buck gave them the finger.

"You think it's smart to antagonize an A.D.A.?"

He shrugged. "My lawyer's the best in the state. He won't be able to keep me outta prison, but eventually I'll be paroled, and when I am, I've been promised Easy Street."

Devon nodded. "We've got two witnesses connecting Zeb to the crime."

"Zeb who?"

"Remember stopping at the Exxon in Artesia?"

Buck shrugged.

"A mechanic identified Zeb as the one pumping gas while you ran interference. We also have an I.D. from the man who sold Zeb the Pontiac."

"So my rich cousin gave me a car. Big deal."

"The big deal is that Nathan was stabbed six times in the chest with an ice pick. After that, the killer stabbed him five more times in the back."

Buck stuck his top lip out and tucked his bottom one tight underneath it.

"Then he strangled Nathan with electrical cord."

Buck stared at the table.

"Anyone capable of doing that is carrying a lot of rage bottled up inside. You don't strike me as having that much anger."

Buck met his eyes.

"The man who does will kill again. If you let him go, you'll be as much of an accomplice then as you are now."

Buck kept quiet.

"When and if you get paroled," Devon said, "you might be his next victim."

"Way I figure, the chances of that are pretty much equal 'tween then and now."

"Not if you help us put him where he belongs."

"He'll get his in the winds of karma."

Devon sighed. "Maybe that's true, but we can't run society leaving vengeance to God."

"Then we'll never run it right."

Devon stood up and held out his hand. "Good luck."

Buck squinted suspiciously. "Why're you wishing me luck?"

"Figure you'll need it."

Buck slowly stood up and looked at the hand offered in friendship. Stretching the maximum reach of the chain holding his manacles to his waist, he accepted the gesture with as much grace as he could muster.

In late afternoon, the wind picked up, stripping the trees of all remaining color. Amy sat nestled deep in the pit of her inflatable plastic chair, staring out the window at the mulberry waving its now bare branches against the darkening sky. Her mother had wanted to stay with her, but Amy insisted she needed time alone. Wallowing in the dregs of sorrow, she relived the last moments of Nathan's life, wondering if he had thought of her.

She knew only that he had been killed shortly after leaving school. She didn't know where or how, and a morbid part of her curiosity wished she could savor every detail as her last chance to share a few more minutes with the boy she knew she would always love more deeply than any other. Even now, within the first hours of her bereavement, she understood why her mother had never married. No mere man could hope to measure up to the purity of a boy lost in his last moment of innocence. Forever she would see him offering his hand to help her, and she would forever remember how she had jumped into the future alone. Her intention had been to prove her strength to stand on equal ground. Now, weakened by his loss, she longed to return to that moment and stand in his shadow.

Her memories were all she was left with, along with the unadorned fact of his having been taken from school and driven to his execution. She hoped he hadn't guessed what would happen, that he had enjoyed some aspect of the scenery along the way. But in the end, he must have known. How long had it taken? Had he known why and maybe cursed her for having caused it?

She rested her forehead against her knees, thinking of her mother in the kitchen washing the cups and spoons left in the sink, and of the love so strong between them, especially now when the hurt was so blatant and the yearning to heal so strong. Realizing that what she received from her mother was what she craved to give Nathan, she decided all love was the same, flowing through people everywhere, living or dead.

And those left out? What could she say about them? The people who gave no love because they had received none. People like Zeb. Or his mother, whom Amy had seen in the school office that morning. Alicia Mulroney in her nubby silk jacket the color of fresh cream in the sun, her snug charcoal skirt over her slim hips and long legs, her crisp haircut and artfully done face, not hiding her baffled eyes. Did her feelings for her son have any bearing on what Lucinda felt for her daughter? And Zeb, how was he feeling? Was he proud of himself? Or was he kneeling in the agony of remorse?

She raised her head and looked at her blue phone on a low shelf of her bookcase. Hearing the screen door open and close, she watched her mother walk out under the mulberry to sit at the picnic table beneath the tree's swaying branches. Her mother's short auburn hair fluttered in the wind, her jacket puffed and fell with the gusts as she sat with her back to the house, leaning on the table with her elbows, perfectly still except for the wind.

Amy was surprised she remembered, but when she lifted the phone his number came to her mind and she punched it in, feeling as if she were moving in a trance. At the other end, the phone rang twice, then was picked up by someone who didn't speak, though she could hear him breathing. After a moment, she whispered his name and felt his surprise.

"Is it you?"

"Yes," she said.

They breathed in unison, then she asked, "Did you do it?"

"I want to see you."

Tears ran down her cheeks. "Will you tell me about it?"

"Not on the phone."

"Where?"

When he told her, she hung up and walked out to the picnic table. "I'm hungry," she said. "Will you fix me something to eat?"

Lucinda smiled. "What would you like?"

"Anything." She shrugged. "Long as it's hot."

She sat down as her mother walked away, and she waited for her mother to become engrossed in the task before she stood up and walked to the door of Devon's apartment. It was locked, so she lifted the last brick on the left of the flower garden and found the spare key. She knew her mother could look out any minute, but she left it to fate whether or not she would be interrupted. Safely inside, she smiled to think fate was on her side. In the third drawer she searched, she found his gun in its shoulder holster. Awkwardly she struggled into the contraption, then perused his closet for a jacket she could wear without looking ridiculous. She chose a lightweight yellow windbreaker, zipping it halfway up and pulling it down past her hips.

Outside again, she didn't bother to look toward the house. If her mother was meant to stop her, it would happen. But it didn't. She walked down the driveway and turned north. Around the corner, she jogged into the alley where she found a bicycle beside an open garage. As she pedaled fiercely toward the pecan grove, she remembered regretting having put herself in Buck's car, and she wondered if she would regret what she was doing now. She decided that to live without knowing would be worse than taking this risk.

Zeb was waiting at the forty-eighth sluice, his red Spyder parked in the variegated shadows under the trees. From any vantage point, the severely pruned orchard looked like oversized twigs parading in perfectly aligned columns to infinity. She leaned her bike against the nearest tree and faced him across the dancing shadows while the wind clapped the bare branches as if in erratic applause.

He wore a blue shirt and gray trousers, his hands in his pockets as he watched her.

"Nice jacket," he quipped.

"I pinched it. The bike, too."

He laughed. "I could've picked you up."

She looked at his car. "Did you take him in that?"

A teasing smile split his lips. "How do I know you're not wearing a wire?"

She shrugged, then admitted, "It never occurred to me."

He laughed again. "What do you want?"

"To know why you did it."

"I'm not saying anything till you prove you're not wearing a wire."

"How can I do that?"

"Let me search you."

She took a step away.

"Let me see under your coat."

221

Slowly she unzipped the jacket and carefully pulled the windbreaker open just enough that the gun was still hidden in the billow of the sleeve.

He came close, smiling as his hands explored her waist all around, her abdomen as high as the edge of her bra, down her tummy to where the zipper on her jeans stopped, then he rested his hands on her hips. "Guess not."

She smiled bravely, knowing the holster fit so loosely its tip hung barely above his hand.

"Know what I wish?" he asked.

She shook her head.

"I wish I'd videotaped it. I could show it to you if I had."

"Why did you do it?"

"If I promise to tell, will you kiss me?"

She nodded. He slanted his head and touched her lips with his, nibbling a moment, then thrusting with his tongue. When he finally pulled back with satisfaction, she swallowed, wanting to spit.

He lifted the opening of her jacket as if to belittle its fit, and in so doing revealed the brown leather strap across her shoulder. He opened the jacket wider and saw the pistol beneath her arm. "Who's that for?"

"Nobody," she said, trying to step out of his hands.

He pulled her closer, his grip on her waist. "Did you come here to shoot me?"

She shook her head.

He backed her against a tree, the trunk hard on her spine. "That's so cool, Amy. Goddamn if you aren't the best girl! Let's get married. You're eighteen, aren't you?"

She shook her head.

"We'll lie. Nobody can stop us. I can do anything I please! You know what Ol' Zeb said about it? Said he'd sweep it under the carpet so the citizens won't know what they're walking on! Wasn't that a great way to put it? With him on my side, there's no limit to what I can do!"

"Why did you do it?" she asked, her voice almost breaking.

He smiled, pinning her against the tree with his body. "It made me hot," he whispered. "I'm getting that way again just thinking about it."

She sobbed, struggling to breathe.

"Want to know what his last words were?"

She nodded, the bark scrabbling against the back of her head, her face wet with tears.

"Ow!" He laughed. "Not very poetic, was it? Course I was stabbing him with an ice pick, so I don't guess he was at his best."

She squeezed her eyes shut.

Suddenly he let go and she felt the weight of the gun leave the holster as he stepped away. When she opened her eyes, he was examining the pistol, his face aglow.

"A 9-millimeter Beretta! I wouldn't've expected you to have such a sophisticated weapon."

"It's not mine," she said, her voice ragged. "I borrowed it."

"From who?"

A shadow shifted in the trees behind him. An antelope or deer maybe, or a stray dog. "A friend," she said. "I have to return it."

"I don't think you're gonna get that chance." He raised the gun in both hands, aimed at her. "Since you won't marry me, I have to kill you now that you know. But it'll be a shame if you die a virgin."

She heard a whir in the air, then a moldy two-by-four came out of nowhere and smacked the side of his face. His head spun as his hands fell limp and the gun slithered into the dank mulch covering the ground. Zeb fell sideways, then struggled to his knees. The board hit the back of his head, and blood flowered from his mouth just before he fell flat with a grunt.

Amy looked at the man wielding the board. He was bare-chested, young and unkempt. He held the board in readiness until convinced Zeb wasn't moving, then slowly turned to look at her.

"Who are you?" she whispered.

"You okay?"

She nodded. "Is he dead?"

He shrugged. "You wanta find out?"

She shook her head.

He walked over to where the gun was half-buried. Only after he had picked it up did he drop the board. Then he studied the gun. "Is it ready to fire?"

"I don't know."

He aimed it at Zeb anyway and cautiously approached. Kneeling, he put his finger beneath one bloody nostril. After a long moment, he stood up and backed away, came close and pushed the gun into her hands. "Get outta here."

"What about you?"

He walked behind a tree where he picked up a shirt and put it on, though it was wet. "I just came to wash in the ditch 'fore catching a bus." He pulled on a filthy jacket and shrugged into a backpack with a sleeping bag tied to the bottom. "If we both go about our business, nobody'll ever know we were here."

She looked at Zeb. "What about him?"

"He won't tell."

Taking hold of her arm, he propelled her toward the bike. "Go on. I'll mess up your tracks on my way out."

She slid the gun into its holster and swung on, then ped-aled fast, concentrating on keeping her balance as she sped along the lane. When she reached the edge of the orchard, she stopped and looked back at the drifter smudging her tracks with his feet. Beneath the striated shadows, the silhouette of him with his pack looked like some cumbersome bison from a time long before anyone ever thought to plant trees on this prairie.

Devon found Lucinda at the picnic table when he got home. The grass was pale in the moonlight, a smooth manicured expanse, as he sat down across from her.

"I'm glad you're back," she said. "Amy was gone a little bit ago, and for a while I thought I was going to spend the rest of my life alone."

"Where'd she go?"

"For a walk, is what she said."

He nodded, suppressing his curiosity for her sake. "I mowed the lawn yesterday."

"I've been admiring it."

They smiled at each other, comfortably sharing their melancholy.

Softly she asked, "How long had you known he was dead?"

"I was pretty sure from the beginning."

"Why? Killing him was so senseless."

"Yeah, but only a sentimentalist could have expected a happy ending."

"And you're not sentimental, are you, Devon?"

He shook his head. "How do you feel about what I am?"

She sighed. "I'd like you to ask me again in a while."

"What'll we do in the meantime?"

"We could start by watching TV with Amy. I don't think she'll be able to sleep for a while yet."

"What's a teenager watch these days?" he asked as they walked toward the house.

"It was MTV just before I came out."

He slid his arm around her waist. "Maybe we can listen to the radio in the kitchen."

"Maybe," she agreed.

Between gaps in the television noise, Amy heard them come in and tune the radio to an easy listening station. A few minutes later she heard the soft shuffling of their feet and knew they were dancing. She stayed put until finally someone went to the bathroom, then she walked into the kitchen and found Devon alone. Only the light in the oven was on, coating the room with a cozy glow. When a song she vaguely knew started playing, she held out a hand, inviting him to dance.

He felt different than Nathan, more solid and reliable, though she told herself she was being unfair. It wasn't Nathan's fault he wasn't still with her. Devon was also a much better dancer than Nathan had been, guiding her so smoothly she felt they were moving inside a dream. As she fought against crying, thinking of all that Nathan would never learn, she felt Devon kiss the top of her head. She leaned her cheek against his shirt until she felt in control again, then met his eyes. "I know now how you feel."

He smiled. "About what?"

"Having killed someone."

He stood still, his face a frown of concern.

"Sometimes," she said, "it's the only way to stop them. Know what I mean?"

He nodded, and she laid her cheek against his shirt and started them dancing again. Close to her ear he said gently, "But don't do it, Amy."

She shook her head and promised, "I won't." Then, so softly only the dead could be expected to hear, she whispered, "It's been done."

Epilogue

Rene Donnor, the school secretary on the day Nathan Wheeler was kidnapped, retired to work as a volunteer in her church's pre-school. Tom Barrow, the vice principal, resigned and moved out of state, leaving Charles Shane, the principal who had been in Socorro that day, to face the public outcry. The district at first denied that the vice principal had failed to ask for identification, but the police department was anxious to reassure everyone that the imposter had not possessed even counterfeit credentials. After details of the department's investigation appeared in the newspaper, the district admitted the truth.

Nathan's birth parents sued for wrongful death and negligence of duty. It was a condition of their settlement that the amount not be disclosed. Both of them attended his funeral, loving in death the boy they'd had no time for in life. His foster family was also there, as well as two hundred students from Berrendo High. Amy Sterling, whose identity as Nathan's girlfriend had been unsuccessfully concealed by the police, was accompanied by her mother and a former police detective from El Paso who, it was rumored, had been instrumental in achieving Buck Powell's arrest.

The death of Zebediah Mulroney II was an odd idiosyncrasy, but the Chief of Police insisted there was no connection between the two crimes. The murder of Li'l Zeb was never solved, no motive discovered and no suspect named. His mother returned to her family in Texas, and it was said the remaining father and son hadn't spoken to each other since her departure.

On trial for the kidnapping and murder of Nathan Wheeler, Buck Powell was represented by Hutch Sylvester, an expensive lawyer from Ruidoso. Rumors abounded as to who was footing the bill, but no speculations appeared in print. The trial lasted a full week and concluded with jury deliberations lasting less than an hour.

He was sentenced to life plus fourteen years, which didn't negate the possibility of parole. Since he pled not guilty, no motive was established. The prosecutor theorized Buck had sought revenge for having been an outcast during his own school years, and several former classmates testified that they had teased him for being a fat nerd. The defense hypothesized that Nathan was abducted as a lark but the actual murder had been committed by a transient while Buck was away getting supper.

Although no one believed in the existence of the homicidal transient, the permeating presence of a ghostly accomplice spared Buck the death penalty and magnified the murder's abiding mystery for local historians and gossips.

Among the latter, Devon Gray's lingering residence in Mrs. Sterling's garage apartment was a topic whose piquancy never dulled.

About the Author

Elizabeth Fackler is the author of novels, short stories, and poetry. Sunstone Press has recently reissued her classic novel on the Lincoln County War: *Billy the Kid: The Legend of El Chivato*. Western Writers of America called it "a magnificent achievement in historical fiction." She lives with her husband, Michael, and their two dogs, Pecos and Mitchum, in Capitán, New Mexico.

FIC FAC

Fackler, Elizabeth.
Endless river.